Nurses to Brides

*The Peniglatt sisters find their
happily-ever-afters when wedding bells ring!*

The Peniglatt sisters
couldn't be more different—
Kira is Miss Responsible, whilst Krissy is
the family wild child! Their only similarity is
their total dedication to caring for others.

These hard-working nurses
don't have much time for love. Until
two very special men walk into their lives,
determined to sweep them off their feet!

The Doctor She Always Dreamed Of

Can Derrick tempt Kira to believe in for ever?

and

The Nurse's Newborn Gift

Will single mum Krissy let Spencer
into her life…and her heart?

You won't want to miss this
sexy and emotional duet
from the fabulous Wendy S. Marcus!

Dear Reader,

I'm thrilled to be back with two brand-new Medical Romances about Kira and Krissy Peniglatt—two very special sisters who work hard to care for and give to others without expecting anything in return.

In *The Doctor She Always Dreamed Of* Kira is a no-nonsense professional, working on the business side of nursing. Rather than enjoying the glitz and glamour of New York City, she divides her time between her job as Director of Case Management at a large insurance carrier and caring for her severely brain-injured mother. With no time to spare, she gave up on finding love a long time ago. But she's never met a man like Dr Derrick Limone—a man willing to do anything to spend time with her.

In *The Nurse's Newborn Gift* Krissy is a laid-back travelling nurse who's in the process of changing her carefree life to keep a promise to her dead best friend—a soldier killed in the war. Having his baby, giving his parents the gift of a grandchild they can dote on and love in his absence, may seem extreme to some—but not to Krissy. She's waited five years, and she's ready to do it all on her own. But Spencer Penn, the baby's godfather, has other ideas.

I hope you enjoy reading Kira's and Krissy's stories as much as I enjoyed writing them! To find out about my other books, visit WendySMarcus.com.

Wishing you all good things,

Wendy S. Marcus

THE NURSE'S NEWBORN GIFT

BY
WENDY S. MARCUS

First published in Great Britain 2016
By Mills & Boon, an imprint of HarperCollins*Publishers*
1 London Bridge Street, London, SE1 9GF

Large Print edition 2017

© 2016 Wendy S. Marcus

ISBN: 978-0-263-06680-7

Our policy is to use papers that are natural, renewable
and recyclable products and made from wood grown
in sustainable forests. The logging and manufacturing
processes conform to the legal environmental
regulations of the country of origin.

Printed and bound in Great Britain
by CPI Antony Rowe, Chippenham, Wiltshire

Wendy S. Marcus is an award-winning author of contemporary romance who lives in the beautiful Hudson Valley region of New York, where she spends way too much time indoors on her computer. Writing. Really! Okay…more like where she spends way too much time on Twitter and Facebook! To learn more about Wendy, and the books she's managed to write in spite of her social media addiction, visit WendySMarcus.com.

Books by Wendy S. Marcus

Mills & Boon Medical Romance

Beyond the Spotlight…
Craving Her Soldier's Touch
Secrets of a Shy Socialite

When One Night Isn't Enough
Once a Good Girl…
The Nurse's Not-So-Secret Scandal
NYC Angels: Tempting Nurse Scarlet

Visit the Author Profile page at millsandboon.co.uk for more titles.

This book is dedicated to my readers.
Thank you for reading and reviewing my books.
I love chatting with you on social media!

With special thanks to my son, who didn't want
to have his name mentioned in one of my books,
for helping me with the athletic training aspects
of this story. Any errors are my own.

Thank you to my wonderful editor,
Flo Nicoll,for always pushing me to do my best.

And thank you to my family,
for supporting me in all that I do.

Praise for
Wendy S. Marcus

'Wendy S. Marcus is a special author for
me… Read this and you'll get an enthralling
contemporary love story.'

—Goodreads on
Craving Her Soldier's Touch

'If you are looking for a read that will have
you laughing, crying and sighing, while being
swept up in sweet yet hot romance, I highly
recommend *Craving Her Soldier's Touch*.'

—Goodreads

'If you are looking for a smart, sexy,
heartwarming contemporary medical romance
that is hard to put down, I highly recommend
you try *Tempting Nurse Scarlet*!'

—Goodreads on
NYC Angels: Tempting Nurse Scarlet

PROLOGUE

KRISSY PENIGLATT REMEMBERED the middle-of-the-night telephone conversation like it'd taken place yesterday as opposed to two years ago. Her best friend in the whole world, Jarrod, had called two days before he was scheduled to deploy for his first tour of duty overseas in the Middle East. A courageous U.S. Army soldier, prepared to give his life for his country, his nineteen-year-old self struggling a bit with the finality of the deed should he be unlucky enough to perish in battle.

"Promise me, if I manage to get myself killed, you'll do it."

He'd been there for her after her father had left when she was ten years old and after her mother's attack and subsequent severe traumatic brain injury shortly after she'd turned fourteen. He'd comforted her and consoled her and cheered her up time and time again, year after year, asking for and expecting nothing in return.

Of course, Krissy would do anything he asked of her, anything to put his mind at ease, to keep him focused on staying alive rather than what would happen if he…didn't. But, *"You're not going to get yourself killed,"* she'd told him. The response had been automatic. She'd refused to even consider the possibility of a life without Jarrod in it. They'd been inseparable for over a decade. Sure, her leaving for college and him enlisting in the army right out of high school would change things between them. To be expected. But it was only supposed to be temporary. A few years apart, then they'd be ready to start their adult lives, together.

Well, not *together*, together, but inseparable once again, maybe living in the same apartment building, or in the same town at the very least.

"My mom can't stop crying," Jarrod had said. *"My dad can barely look at me without tearing up."*

They were such a kind and caring couple. An only child, Jarrod's parents' lives revolved around him. No parents loved their son more than Jarrod's parents loved him. Lucky for Krissy that love had extended to Jarrod's best friends as well. On some level, she'd actually felt closer to his parents than to her own. She owed them so much.

"I need to know," he'd said, uncharacteristically emotional, *"if my life is cut short, that some part of me lives on, that my parents have a grandchild to love and spoil. Because losing me..."*

He didn't need to finish. Losing him would be devastating, to his parents and to her.

The anguish in his voice had made her willing to say anything, to *do* anything to make it go away, to bring back the kind, happy, always joking boy she'd loved like a brother. So even though she'd never expected to ever have to follow through, she'd agreed.

"Okay. I'll do it, but only if you manage to get yourself killed, which you aren't going to do, so this conversation is a total waste of time."

A short two years later, twenty-one-year-old Krissy stood all alone, her body feeling weighted down by hundred pound blocks of ice, the chill in her bones in direct contrast to the beautiful, bright sunshiny spring day, as she stared at the casket that held the remains of her best friend in the whole world. The service long over, only a few mourners remained, mulling around over by their cars. But Krissy couldn't bring herself to leave, knowing once she did, the workmen standing off in the distance would lower Jarrod's body into the cold, dark ground, and she'd never again be as close to him as she now stood.

Her heart ached, literally hurt, every time she thought about never seeing him again, never being on the receiving end of one of his powerful hugs, never hearing his annoying snort-laugh that always got her snort-laughing too.

A tear trickled down her cheek.

Who would she share good news with? Who could she count on to cheer her up when she had a bad day? Whose visits and phone calls would give her something to look forward to? Who would ever understand her and love her and accept her, as is, like Jarrod had?

No one.

Out of the corner of her eye, Krissy saw Jarrod's mother, Patti, walking toward her. A quiet, plain woman, with short darkish hair, a figure that tended to run toward chubby, and a heart filled with love, she looked like she'd aged twenty years in the past two. "Come on, honey." She put her arm around Krissy's shoulders and tried to steer her away. "We have a room reserved at a local restaurant. Jarrod wanted a party, so we'll give him a party."

"And it's not a party..." Krissy started.

"Without Mom's caramel, fudge brownies with walnuts for dessert," Patti finished sadly, repeating what Jarrod would have said if he'd been alive and able to talk.

The fact that he wasn't, and never would be again, sent another wave of tears flooding Krissy's raw, sore eyes.

Patti pulled her into a hug, not as wonderful as one of Jarrod's, but close. "I swear that boy could eat a whole pan by himself." She rubbed Krissy's back. "I put a batch in the casket with him," she said quietly, almost numbly. "Along with a picture of the two of you from graduation. Gosh darn it, this is so unfair."

"I know." Krissy squeezed her tight, well acquainted with the unfairness of life.

"Come on, you two," Jarrod's dad, Bart, said. A tall, solid man, like his son, he put a strong arm around each of them. "Time to go." He walked them away from the casket that held her best friend, away from the grave where he would lay for eternity…alone. "He lives on in our hearts," Bart said, walking slowly. "We may not have a piece of him to hold on to, but as long as we think about him and remember him, he'll never be fully gone from our lives."

But they *could* have a piece of him to hold on to, if Krissy did what she'd promised to do.

CHAPTER ONE

Five years and seven and a half months later

KRISSY SAT ON the bed in her temporary bedroom at her sister Kira's house in White Plains, New York, home from a mostly fantastic six-month assignment, that'd actually turned into seven months, in Hawaii, sorting through a mess of papers. She moved the real estate listings into one pile, time to find a place of her own and set down some roots. Help Wanted printouts got their own stack, her days as a traveling nurse over, it was time to figure out what she wanted to do going forward, in a job that would keep her in one place, but no rush on that. For the time being she was happy to work as an office nurse in her soon-to-be brother-in-law's family practice.

That left pictures and mementos of all the fun times she'd had with Zac, her ex-traveling nurse buddy/friend with benefits/almost but not quite a boyfriend. She scooped those up and dumped them in the trash basket on the floor, time to move on.

Krissy had waited long enough. She had a promise to keep.

And Zac, for as often as he'd professed his love for her, which happened pretty regularly after orgasms—back when they used to have sex, before her successful artificial insemination—didn't love her enough to give up his carefree existence to settle down with her and start a family. Especially, he'd made sure to point out, a family that included another man's child.

Which was probably a good thing since Zac was everything Jarrod had hated in Krissy's boyfriends. Stuff that made him fun—he partied hard, didn't take life too seriously, and couldn't care less what people thought of him—would have made him a bad parent. Which is probably why, while their last goodbye had caused some tears— seemed tears came rather easily these days—the ache in her heart had been short-lived.

Krissy found the manila folder she'd been looking for when she'd first gotten the bright idea to dump out the box. The sight of her name written in Jarrod's scrawl still gave her a pang of loss in her chest, bringing on the memory of his funeral, the party afterward, where she'd sat in the back and kept to herself, and the talk she'd had with his parents before heading home.

"He left it all to you," Patti had said, handing Krissy the manila envelope she now held in her hands. *"His savings, some certificates of deposit, and his car. And you're the sole beneficiary on his military life insurance policy."* Patti had stared into Krissy's eyes, looking for answers. One question was obvious: Why would he leave everything to you?

At the time, Krissy couldn't do more than stare right back in bewilderment, shocked and overwhelmed by what Jarrod had done. For her. For the son or daughter he would never know. His confidence that she would do what she'd promised to do had made her love him and miss him even more.

When Krissy had regained her composure, she'd briefly considered telling Jarrod's parents of her promise. But she'd decided against it, wasn't ready to make the commitment, or to get their hopes up. She'd only been twenty-one years old, for God's sake, just starting out, and in no way ready to have a baby.

But now, at twenty-six, almost twenty-seven years old she felt…ready. Well, as ready as a woman about to become solely responsible for the life of another human being could feel. Sure, it would have been nice to have a man who loved her and was eager to accompany her on this journey, but three boyfriends had been quick to skedaddle upon learning of her plans to have her dead best friend's baby. Fine. She never loved any of them as much as she'd loved Jarrod, anyway. And settling for Zac would have been a horrible mistake. Thank goodness he'd seen that, when she'd been too worried about the responsibility of caring for and raising a child, alone, to see it for herself.

"I *can* do it on my own," she told the baby in her belly, hoping it couldn't sense her self-doubt. "I'm going to be a great mom," she told herself, remembering what a wonderful mother her own mom had been, before the brain injury. If Krissy could manage to be half as wonderful, it'd be enough.

"I *will* do it on my own." She'd given herself five years to mature and prepare. Five years to travel and have fun and live life to its fullest before settling down to raise her child. Five years to find a man worthy of being her baby's surrogate daddy. Didn't happen.

"Alone is fine." Thanks to Jarrod and years of hard work and careful spending, she had plenty of money. She was used to living independently and had excellent nursing skills, which would surely come in handy during any bouts of baby choking or illness. Not that she planned on having to do everything on her own forever.

Surely Jarrod's parents would help with babysitting…if they were still local. She swallowed back the guilt of waiting so long as she opened the large tan envelope and pulled out the letters inside, all but one still sealed, each labeled by Jarrod with specific instructions.

#1—For Krissy—Open after my funeral

She'd read that letter so many times she could recite it from memory.

#2—For Spencer—When you're ready to give it to him

Spencer, of all people! Why did he want Spencer to be the baby's godfather? Spencer hated her.

And, as of junior year of high school, the feeling was mutual.

#3—For my mom and dad—To explain our agreement

She planned to hand-deliver that one after the birth of the baby.

#4—To my son on his tenth birthday
#4—To my daughter on her tenth birthday

She caressed her pregnant belly, knowing that it would be Jarrod's son who would be getting letter number four on his tenth birthday.

"Stop putting it off." Krissy reached inside to pull out a piece of paper that had Jarrod's parents' home telephone number on it. God willing it hadn't changed. With a deep, fortifying breath, she picked up her cell phone and dialed the number.

First ring.

She twirled the post earring in her left ear, an annoying nervous habit Jarrod would have been sure to point out.

Second ring.

Suddenly parched, she reached for the glass beside her bed and took a sip of water.

Third ring.

She started to plan her message. *Hello Mr. and Mrs. Sadler. It's*—

"Hello?"

Krissy recognized Patti's voice immediately, so familiar it brought on a rush of emotion. She swallowed. Wasn't ready—

"Hello?" Patti said again.

Stop being an idiot. "Hi, Mrs. Sadler," Krissy said. "It's me—"

"Krissy! Oh, my word. How are you, honey? It's been…so long." Patti may have started out happy to hear from Krissy, but the sadness tinged with disappointment and hurt in her 'It's been… so long' was unmistakable.

"I know," Krissy said. "I'm sorry. I…" How did one adequately apologize for failing to keep in touch with a woman who'd been like a mother to her throughout high school? For failing to be there for a woman who had been there for Krissy when her own mother couldn't be? For failing to offer her love and support to a sweet and caring

woman who'd been dealing with the worst trag-
edy a mother could face, the death of a child?

"I..." Krissy tried again. But how could she adequately explain that she'd tried to stay in touch,
and she had, for a good year after Jarrod's death.
But hearing the complete desolation in Patti's
voice during each phone call had been too dif-
ficult? That it made Krissy feel things she didn't
want to feel when she'd been trying so hard to
move past the pain? That knowing she held the
key to Patti and Bart's happiness, in the form of a
grandbaby fathered by their beloved son, but not
feeling ready to give up her freedom to have that
baby at such a young age, made her feel guilty
and selfish and just plain terrible?

"I'm sorry," she said again. It would have to do
until she could explain further.

"I'm sorry, too," Patti said. "I've missed you.
Now tell me everything. What have you been up
to?"

Easy as that, sweet Patti moved past what a terrible friend Krissy had been.

An hour later they were all caught up—getting
caught up on the happenings of Patti and Bart had
taken less than five minutes, because not much

new had happened in their lives. They were in the same apartment, working in the same jobs, still mourning the loss of their son. They were going through the motions of life but not really living. It would have broken Jarrod's heart to know. It made Krissy feel even more awful for waiting so long to give them a grandchild to dote on.

But in six weeks, all that would change. She wanted to tell Patti, wanted to hear the joy in her voice and give her something to finally be happy about, but not yet. Not until Patti could hold a happy, healthy baby in her arms. Mr. and Mrs. Sadler had been through too much, couldn't handle any more sadness if anything were to go wrong with the birth, or God forbid, if the baby wasn't born healthy.

Krissy forced out the question she'd called to ask. "I'm wondering if you know how I can reach Spencer Penn?"

"Of course. Spencer is such a dear. He stops by for Sunday dinner every couple of months."

Shoot. Leave it to Spencer to screw up her plans. "I thought he was living out in California. Wasn't that why he hadn't attended Jarrod's funeral?"

"Oh, no. He was only out there for a week or

two, taking his sister to look at colleges. I told him not to cancel his plans that Jarrod would understand. Now hold on a minute. Let me get his number from my address book."

Take all the time you need. Can't find it? No worries. Krissy was in no rush. She'd already put this off longer than she probably should have.

"Here it is." Patti read off the number. "If you don't mind me asking, why do you need it?"

Because your son has a sick sense of humor and I'm trying to do the right thing and abide by his wishes for Spencer to be our baby's godfather, even though the thought made her a bit nauseous.

"I was under the impression," Patti went on, "that the two of you weren't friends anymore."

No. They weren't. Not since that night… "I need to talk to him about something important," was all Krissy said, hoping Patti would leave it at that.

Thank goodness she did. "Don't be a stranger," Patti said. "If you have some time, we'd love to see you."

Soon, if things went as planned, they'd be seeing quite a lot of her. "I'd like that. I'll be in touch." After your grandson is born.

* * *

A week later, on a Friday evening after work, Krissy sat in her parked car, watching the clock, not wanting to show up too early. She'd kept the heat on, because an April evening in New York was not near as warm as an April evening in Hawaii. Or maybe it was nerves giving her a chill.

It'd taken days of back and forth messages to set up a meeting with Spencer, the pain in the butt. He kept suggesting various bars in White Plains, all relatively close to where she worked, saying a neutral location with lots of witnesses was safest for both of them. Seemed the years hadn't managed to mature him any.

Regardless of the fact she wasn't drinking any alcohol these days, the topic they needed to discuss would be better dealt with in private. So Krissy had insisted on meeting him at his apartment—which, as it turned out, was also relatively close to where she worked.

Learning that had been a bit unsettling.

The christening, the confirmation, and maybe a few milestone birthday parties was all the time she'd planned to have to tolerate Spencer. The bare minimum required for her son to get to know his godfather. Heaven forbid Spencer wanted to play a bigger role in her child's life.

No. Tonight she'd set some ground rules.

Krissy eyed the clock then the distance between her parking spot and the front door of Spencer's fancy high rise. Six minutes should do it, only because she wasn't walking all that fast these days.

At seven o'clock, on the dot, Krissy knocked on Spencer's door.

A few seconds later, it opened and ho-lee cow. The years had been good to the now very handsome Spencer Penn. He must have grown a foot since high school. His lean, teenage soccer player physique? Gone, replaced by muscles, defined, sexy, desirable muscles that were prominent beneath the short-sleeved black polo shirt and tight fitting khaki pants he wore. His thick, wavy, always mussed—in a lead singer of a boy band kind of way—dark hair? Gone, replaced by a short-ish, surprisingly appealing, buzz cut. His smooth, boyish face? Gone, replaced by sculpted cheekbones, sexy scruff, and full, kissable lips...that were smiling as part of a 'You like what you see?' expression.

Shoot. Krissy focused in on his light brown

eyes, smart eyes that, like Jarrod's, could always seem to tell what she was thinking.

Spencer looked her up and down his gaze settling on her midsection, "Still have a sweet tooth I see."

Any attraction she may have been feeling vanished. Poof! Gone. "Can you manage to *not* be obnoxious, for at least the next five minutes?" If she'd cared one bit what Spencer thought of her, she'd have changed out of her work scrubs and freshened her makeup or run some gel through her short hair. But she didn't care. Krissy handed him Jarrod's letter. "This is why I'm here. And I have no intention of standing out in the hallway like an annoying salesman while you read it. So either invite me in or I'm gone."

Without saying a word, he stepped aside and Krissy walked into his apartment. Feeling awkward, and not wanting to stand there while he read Jarrod's letter, Krissy asked, "Where's your bathroom?"

Spencer looked up from the envelope he'd been staring at but hadn't yet opened and pointed down the hallway to the right. So that's where Krissy headed.

Since she had some time to kill to make her visit believable, she spent it snooping. One toothbrush in the holder. Basic man stuff neatly stashed in the medicine cabinet. An electric beard trimmer. Deodorant. A small box of condoms. Mostly empty drawers. No tampons, or hair paraphernalia, or any signs the same woman visited on a regular basis. Rather than think too hard on why that made her happy, Krissy flushed the toilet, washed her hands, and walked back into the hallway.

Seeing Spencer sitting at the kitchen table, fully engrossed by his letter, Krissy took a few minutes to admire his apartment, neat, modern, and nicely furnished in tans and blacks, so different from the cluttered, messy bedroom of his youth. In the living room he had a bunch of thick textbooks stacked on a low shelf. Krissy walked closer. Anatomy and Physiology. Nutrition. Relaxation. Strength and Conditioning. Athletic Training.

Then she saw it, at eye level, a full color picture of the three of them in a plain black frame, Jarrod on one side, Spencer on the other, and Krissy in the middle. It'd been taken in Central Park, during the winter. They'd been all smiles, with red cheeks, disheveled hats and coats, and covered in snow. Happier times. The good old days, always together…until junior year, when everything had changed.

Beside it were a bunch of pictures of Spencer wearing the same clothes he wore now, posing with various adult male soccer players. "What's with all these soccer pictures?"

"I'm an assistant athletic trainer with the NYC United," he answered, his eyes never leaving the letter. "A semi-pro, United Soccer League team."

Pretty cool, but she'd never tell *him* that. Krissy remembered her sister Kira telling her there was a semi-pro soccer team in their area. They practiced and played at one of the local colleges, which explained why Spencer now lived so close to her. "That's what you went to school for?"

"Got my master's degree in it."

"What does an assistant athletic trainer do exactly?"

"Athletic trainers deal with prevention, acute care and rehabilitation of sports injuries."

Other pictures caught her attention. Spencer hiking. Spencer skiing. Spencer on the beach with a bunch of his good looking friends. *My God!*

Krissy looked away. "No pictures of your girl-friend?"

"I don't have a girlfriend."

Good to know.

Why is that good to know?

Hmmm.

Before she could come up with an answer, Spencer interrupted.

"You're pregnant?" he yelled from the kitchen, in a tone that seemed to indicate women like Krissy shouldn't procreate. Really, he felt it necessary to yell? The apartment wasn't all that big.

"Yes," Krissy said, keeping her voice uninterested and her back to him as she perused the other pictures on the shelf. "Sorry you wasted a perfectly good insult."

"With Jarrod's baby?" he asked.

The disbelief in his tone had her swinging around to face him. "Yes with Jarrod's baby."

From where he sat, Spencer looked up from the letter. "How do I know?"

"How do you know *what*?"

He stood. "How do I know that's Jarrod's baby in here," he motioned to her belly, "and not some other guy's?" He walked closer. "How do I know you didn't get yourself knocked up and now you're digging out these letters Jarrod left you so you can get me, Patti and Bart involved so you don't have to raise the kid on your own? Do they know?"

A rage like she hadn't felt in years, quite possibly since the last time she'd seen Spencer, surged through her. How dare he insinuate… "As if I would waste one minute looking for you if Jarrod hadn't asked me to. As if I would want someone like you in my life, in my baby's life, if Jarrod hadn't specifically stated he wanted you to be his baby's godfather. God I hate you. This was a mistake." She stomped toward the door. "I don't know what Jarrod was thinking." She bent to pick up her pocketbook—no easy task considering she'd soon be entering her ninth month of pregnancy, but no way would she ask Spencer for help. "And, no, Patti and Bart don't know. Not yet. I'm waiting until after the baby's born. To save them from worry…or having to grieve another loss if something goes wrong."

"Wait," he said, sounding tired.

No way would she wait simply because he wanted her to. But she could slow down long enough to let him have it. "You may not believe this is Jarrod's baby, and frankly, I don't care whether you do or you don't. I did what he asked me to do, out of love for him, but I won't—"

"Love." Spencer let out a cruel laugh. "You don't know the meaning of the word. If you loved Jarrod so much, why'd you flirt with him and tease and then flaunt all your boyfriends in front of him?"

Yes, she'd teased and joked. But she most certainly had not flirted with Jarrod. "I did not—"

Apparently ready for a fight, he set his hands on his hips and leaned in. "Oh, yes, you did. Holding their hands in front of him, sucking face in front of him, telling him the intimate details of your sex life, breaking his heart over and over again."

Breaking his heart? "I did not break his heart. We were pals, best friends. We talked about everything." Although to be honest, usually Krissy had done most of the talking while Jarrod had done most of the listening.

"He didn't want to be your best friend. At least that's not *all* he wanted to be. I never understood how you couldn't see it? Except that you were always too absorbed in yourself and what was going on in your life to notice much about anyone else."

Even though that had been true, Krissy told him

to, "Go to hell." She didn't want to relive those days. She'd moved on. She was a better person now. She was doing the right thing by having Jarrod's baby, following through with his wishes. But she refused to stand here and listen to one more word out of Spencer's mouth. She turned to the door.

"All the times you ran to him when you were upset, cried on his shoulder, let him hold you and console you. You gave him just enough to keep him content with the scraps of affection you tossed in his direction, to make him hopeful that maybe someday…"

"Shut up." Krissy's chest started to ache.

"He loved you," Spencer said. "Boyfriend, girlfriend loved you."

No.

"But you came after me." His words dripped with resentment. "Kissed me on some whim, without a care who saw you, without a care for my friendship with Jarrod or how much it would hurt him if he found out."

"What's the matter, Krissy?" Spencer had said to her that night. *"Getting desperate? Every other guy at the party turned you down?"* Like she was

a common slut, like she'd only gone after him because no one else would have her. He had no idea how long it'd taken her to finally act on her feelings for him. If anyone had gotten hurt that night it'd been her.

Krissy turned back around to face him. "Jarrod and I were friends. Best friends. That's all."

"He wanted more." Spencer stared her down. "Why do you think he kissed you?"

An innocent peck on the lips, in the tenth grade, beneath the bleachers at a basketball game. "He said he liked me better than any other girl at school and he just wanted to see..." But there'd been nothing. No tingle. No spark. No desire to take the kiss deeper, for either of them...or so she'd thought...so he'd led her to believe. Why?

"Did you have to laugh afterward?" Spencer asked, doing nothing to hide his contempt, as he walked back to the kitchen, folded Jarrod's letter and stuffed it back in the envelope.

The whole kiss thing had made her feel weird and out of sorts. So yeah, she'd laughed. A nervous kind of laugh, because she didn't know what else to do, the two them standing there, alone... "He told you about that?"

Spencer nodded. Then he shrugged. "You confided in him and he confided in me. After you went off with your friends, like nothing had happened, he sent me a text." Spencer looked down at his feet. "I found him crying in the third floor bathroom."

"You told me he went home because he wasn't feeling well."

"He *wasn't* feeling well. He was heartbroken. He'd finally kissed the girl he'd secretly loved for years and she'd laughed in his face."

Krissy's stomach churned.

Spencer folded the envelope and slid it into his back pocket, casual as can be, while Krissy felt like the very foundation of her life was crumbling beneath her feet.

"The next day, after he'd calmed down he decided he could be patient." Spencer's eyes met hers. "That you were worth the wait. That eventually he'd win you over, but you didn't make it easy on him, did you?"

Had she really hurt her best friend again and again? God help her. All the things she'd confided in him. Vomit started to creep up to the back of her throat. "I had no idea." Absolutely no idea at all or she never would have—

"Why do you think he went into the army?" Spencer looked at her with such anger, such… hatred. "To impress *you*."

No! "Don't you dare belittle his decision," she jabbed her index finger in Spencer's direction, "his commitment and dedication or how hard he'd worked to get into shape. He enlisted because he wanted to serve his country."

"He enlisted to impress *you*." Spencer shook his head. "There was no talking him out of it, believe me, I tried. After hearing you gush about that Martinez kid who'd joined the marines, Jarrod got it into his head that he'd join the military, too. So you'd gush about *him*. He'd planned to come home a war hero so you'd finally see him as a man."

What? "Are you saying…?" The ache in her chest worsened. The floor seemed to undulate beneath her feet. Krissy grabbed on to the wall for stability. "He joined the military because of me?" A sharp pain stabbed at the right side of her belly. "Ow." She rubbed the area, tears forming in her eyes. It couldn't be. "That he's dead…" Her whole abdomen tightened uncomfortably. "He's dead…" She couldn't breathe. "…because of me?"

Fluid gushed between her legs. "No." She clamped them closed.

"What's wrong?" Spencer ran toward her. He looked down. Then he ran back to the kitchen, grabbed a chair and ran back. "Sit."

She wanted to yell, "I am not a dog," because Spencer brought out the fight in her. But if she didn't sit right then there was a good chance she'd collapse to the floor. "I can't have this baby. Not yet." She rubbed her belly, wasn't ready. "It's too soon." The baby kicked. At least that was a good sign.

Krissy could hear Spencer talking but she paid no attention to what he was saying, thoughts of Jarrod swirling in her head. He'd gone into the army because of her. He'd been killed because of her. *I'm sorry. So sorry.*

Spencer knelt down beside her. "How far along are you?"

"I'm due in five weeks." He repeated what she'd told him into his cell phone. "Who are you talking to?"

"An ambulance is on the way."

CHAPTER TWO

UPON THEIR ARRIVAL at the hospital, the ambulance crew whisked them right up to the Labor and Delivery floor where Spencer stood by helplessly—something he was not used to and did not like one bit—while the doctor examined Krissy and the nurse hooked her up to a fetal monitor. Forty-five minutes later, they were alone, Spencer sitting in a guest chair, holding on to a black and white sonogram picture. Krissy in a hospital gown, lying on her side in the bed, facing away from him. The sound of her baby's rapid heartbeat—correction: her *and Jarrod's* baby's rapid heartbeat—filled the tense silence between them.

What had Jarrod been thinking, asking someone as irresponsible and self-centered as Krissy to have his baby, especially when he wouldn't be here to, at the very least, keep an eye on her? And now he expected Spencer to do it? He shifted in the uncomfortable plastic chair. Friendship had limits. Even after death.

Ten years.

For the past ten years, since his father had collapsed on a subway platform and died of a massive heart attack when Spencer was only seventeen, he'd been the man of the family, helping his mother, looking out for his two younger sisters. Finally, just this year, with Reagan in graduate school out in California, Tara finishing her first year of college in Massachusetts, and Mom moved out of their old apartment and into a smaller, more affordable one close to her new boyfriend, he'd earned his freedom.

He had his own place, outside of New York City where his mother still lived, could come and go as he pleased without having to check in with anyone. In the off season he could spend the winter skiing in Utah or on the beach in the Caribbean. Or he could do both! He was responsible for no one but himself...finally.

And now this. Krissy was having a baby, and Jarrod expected Spencer to look after them both? He wanted to run from the room screaming, *Nooooooooooo*.

Seeing her for the first time since high school— her face fuller, but still beautiful, the blue eyes that used to haunt his teenage dreams, her breasts looking even more voluptuous beneath her baggy scrubs—had been like a punch to the gut. And the way she'd been looking him over, with lust in her eyes.

Why couldn't she have looked at him like that back in high school? Why couldn't she have set Jarrod straight all those years ago? Told him, in no uncertain terms, that they'd never be more than friends? Then Jarrod could have gotten a real girl-friend and he wouldn't have gone into the army and he wouldn't be dead! Long buried anger, frustration, and blame had resurfaced. He'd wanted to hurt her, like she'd hurt Jarrod, so many times, like she'd hurt him. So Spencer had emptied the load he'd been carrying, telling her everything.

It was as if nine years had not gone by, as if he hadn't changed at all. As if he was still the antagonistic jerk he'd turned into all those years ago.

But this evening's little bit of bad behavior aside, he *had* changed. He was more tolerant and understanding, at least he tried to be…usually. Now, when he wanted something, he went after it, re-gardless of who else wanted it.

Maybe she had changed, too, at least a little. While the girl she'd been wouldn't have thought twice about making an empty promise to her best friend, old Krissy probably wouldn't have made good on that promise, especially when it involved something as huge and life altering as getting pregnant and having a baby on her own.

That Jarrod had gone as far as to ask wasn't as much of a shock as Krissy agreeing, and actually following through, especially with Jarrod gone. Their agreement could have died with him. No one would have known.

She could have taken all the money Jarrod had left her—a decision that finally made sense—and lived quite comfortably without having to work. Yet she hadn't. According to Jarrod's mom, Krissy had said she'd been working as a traveling nurse. Maybe she wasn't the conniving opportunist he'd thought her to be all these years.

A nicely dressed woman in a pair of killer heels hurried into the room. Tall and thin, the opposite of Krissy, but with the same blue eyes and dark hair, only hers was long and up in a ponytail, it had to be Krissy's sister, Kira. "My, God." She walked past the foot of the bed to the side Krissy was facing. "Are you okay? The baby? What happened?"

A tall man with dark hair followed her in. "Give her a chance to answer."

Whereas Kira didn't notice Spencer, the man with her held out his hand. "Derrick Limone, Kira's fiancé."

According to Jarrod's mom, Krissy had mentioned working for her future brother-in-law, the doctor, at Limone Family Practice. Spencer liked that the man didn't throw his title around. "Spencer Penn." Spencer shook his hand. Then, feeling the need to justify his presence, without admitting to most likely being the reason for Krissy's trip to the hospital, he added, "Baby's godfather."

"Spencer Penn?" Kira asked, and not fondly. "From high school?"

Yeah, *that* Spencer Penn.

Krissy turned onto her back and struggled to sit up.

Without giving it a second thought, Spencer rushed over to help her, for the first time noticing how tired she looked. No wonder. According to what she'd told the doctor and nurse, she'd just recently returned from an assignment in Hawaii, was already working full time while in the process of looking for an apartment, and had not yet had time to visit a local OB-GYN or attend a birthing class.

For a woman as pregnant as Krissy, shouldn't finding a local OB-GYN and attending a birthing class have been the first two things she'd done upon arriving in the area where she'd be having her baby?

"What are you doing here?" Krissy asked Kira.

"A nurse called me."

"Why did a nurse call you? I didn't ask a nurse to call you." She directed her question and statement to Kira. But she directed one heck of a look at Spencer.

Yes. He'd asked the nurse to call Krissy's sister. A woman, in the hospital, possibly about to lose her baby would *want* her sister with her, wouldn't she? Based on the look she'd given him, apparently not.

"Why did a nurse call me?" Kira said. "Maybe because my sister is in the hospital and couldn't be bothered to call me herself, that's why. What happened?"

"Don't look so worried," Krissy said to Kira. "I'm fine."

"You are not fine," Kira said, her eyes roaming over the fetal monitor reading then up to the cardiac monitor. "I told you to get in to see a local OB-GYN as soon as possible."

"Exactly!"

Krissy shot him a glare so fierce it would have burned all the flesh from his face, if such a thing were possible. Okay, so he probably should have kept his opinion to himself. *You're just screwing up left and right today, aren't you?*

To his surprise, rather than lay into him, Krissy turned to Kira and calmly said, "I didn't call because I didn't want you to worry. I didn't want you to drop everything and run over here, which is exactly what I knew you'd do." She reached out and held Kira's hand. "Between managing Derrick's office and helping Tippy care for Mom and being pregnant yourself, you have enough to deal with. I told you I could do this on my own and I will."

A snippet from Jarrod's letter flashed in his mind.

Krissy will try to do everything on her own, but she can't. She'll need help. And since I'm not there, I expect you, my oldest and best friend, my blood brother since the third grade, to be there for her.

"I don't want to be another burden," Krissy went on.

"You're not a burden," Kira said. "You have never been a burden. You're my sister and I love you." She bent down to hug Krissy.

Krissy hugged her back. "I love you, too. And I *did* listen to you. I visited my doctor in Hawaii the day before I left. He examined me and said everything was fine. He recommended to follow up in two to three weeks. I've been researching doctors and asking around. As luck would have it, the doctor who saw me today was one of the ones I was considering. He's agreed to take me on as a patient. So there, you see?" She lifted her hands off of the bed. "No need for you to worry about me."

Then she whipped her evil eyes back to Spencer. "Now that my sister's here, you can go." Krissy dismissed him. "She'll give me a ride home."

"But the doctor—" Spencer tried.

"Don't." The about-to-commit-murder expression she gave him softened when she turned to look at Derrick. "You'll talk to the doctor," she said sweetly, "and get him to let me go home tonight, won't you Derrick?"

"Why wouldn't he let you go home tonight?" Kira asked, obviously worried.

"Because she came in hypertensive," Spencer answered.

"It's not a big deal," Krissy said to Kira. "Really. As if all the hideous and uncomfortable changes your body goes through during pregnancy aren't enough, a new fun fact I learned today, is that when your baby gets to be a certain size, he can kick your bladder and make you pee yourself and think your water's broken and you're going into early labor. I panicked. That's all. My blood pressure shot up and now it's back down. It's been stable throughout my pregnancy. Today was a fluke, a one-time response to an upsetting event."

She'd failed to mention the sharp pain and resulting abdominal tightness she'd felt just prior to her thinking her water had broken. This time he kept quiet. But even that didn't save him.

"Part of the reason I came in hypertensive," she

said to Spencer, looking like she was trying very hard to stay in control, "is because *you* made me go hypertensive." She jabbed her index finger in his direction. "The doctor said I need to stay calm and I can't stay calm when you're here because every time you open your mouth you upset me. Now get out of here." She pointed to the door rather aggressively. "Before you make me burst a blood vessel in my head and have a stroke and you kill me *and* my baby."

Spencer couldn't help it. He crossed his arms over his chest and smiled. "Still have a flair for the dramatic, I see."

Krissy threw her plastic cup of water at him. Luckily she had lousy aim. And there wasn't much water in it.

"On a serious note." Derrick took on what Spencer figured was his Dr. Limone voice. When he had everyone's attention, he pointed at Krissy's cardiac monitor.

Her heart rate and blood pressure, which had, in fact, returned to within normal limits soon after she'd learned her baby was okay, were both back on the rise. Riling her up in high school had provided him with hours of entertainment. Riling her up when she was pregnant and in the hospital? He needed to be more careful. "I'm sorry," he said, forcing as much sincerity as he could into his tone, because he *was* sorry, for real, and for more than teasing her in that moment.

"Why is he even here?" Kira asked. "What would make you pick Spencer Penn, of all people, to be your baby's godfather?" She looked over at him. "No offense, Spencer. But last I remember, Krissy didn't think all that highly of you."

She probably didn't think all that highly of him now, either. Justifiably so.

"Because that's what Jarrod wanted," Krissy said.

"Jarrod?" Kira asked. "What's he got to do with this?"

"This is his baby." Krissy caressed her large belly over the monitor straps, looking down at it, her expression soft and loving and so unexpected, as was the warmth that spread through him when he saw it. "A little boy," she said, with a small smile. "Not to jinx anything, but I've already decided to name him Jarrod Junior and call him J.J."

J.J. Spencer liked it. Jarrod would have liked it too.

He imagined a little boy with Jarrod's mischievous smile and dimples running around and getting into trouble. Between that little bit of imagery and the baby's heart beating loudly through the monitor, reality gave Spencer a second punch to the gut. Like it or not, Jarrod's baby would soon be coming into the world. And he'd need a good man in his life.

Spencer glanced at the bed, at Krissy's hands in particular. No wedding or engagement ring. Did she already have a man in her life? If so, she didn't call him to tell him she was in the hospital. And she'd put Kira down as her emergency contact.

Not that it mattered. Spencer would be there too. To tell little J.J. all about his dad, to introduce him to the banana splits with chocolate sprinkles his dad had loved, to take him to baseball games and introduce him to rock music and teach him all the things he knew Jarrod would want his son to know.

"This is Jarrod's baby?" Kira asked.

Surprising that Krissy hadn't shared that bit of information with her sister.

"Wait a minute," Kira added. "Your artificial

insemination was done with Jarrod's sperm? He had his sperm frozen before he died? And you..."

Krissy nodded.

Spencer had been cruel to insinuate Krissy would try to pass off another man's baby as Jarrod's. Deep down, he didn't believe she'd do such a thing. But Kira mentioning Krissy's artificial insemination put an immediate halt to any lingering question he may have had.

Krissy yawned, a big, totally exhausted looking yawn. "I'll tell you everything. Later. I promise." She repositioned herself in the bed. "Right now, I really need to close my eyes for a few minutes." She found the bed controller and lowered the head of the bed.

"I'm going to go track down her doctor," Derrick said as he left the room.

"I'm going to go grab a cup of coffee," Spencer said, knowing Kira would be in the room if Krissy should need anything. But when he left the room, he didn't go to grab a cup of coffee. He followed Derrick, hoping to listen in on his conversation with Krissy's doctor.

CHAPTER THREE

ON MONDAY MORNING, Krissy sat at the reception desk at Derrick's office, helping Sara with answering phones and checking in/checking out patients, while Kira covered most of her nursing duties in the back. It was that or use a valuable sick day to stay home alone and rest, which would no doubt give her too much time to think about all she had to do before the baby came and worry about the actual giving birth part, which would be anything but restful. So Krissy had given in and agreed to Kira's terms.

The good news, she was getting paid. With her delivery date fast approaching, every penny counted. Working the desk wasn't so bad. And since Kira had been spending her time on the business side of nursing for the past few years, prior to taking on the job of office manager at Derrick's family practice, her nursing skills were a little rusty, which meant Krissy still got to work with patients who needed injections, blood draws, and/or EKGs.

Krissy had just checked out a mother and her newborn baby following her first checkup when Spencer walked in followed by a thinner but equally fit and equally good looking man. Lord help her. Spencer in khakis and a polo shirt looked good. But Spencer in black dress slacks, a crisp white fitted dress shirt and a black tie was off the chart hot. To the point his hotness was making her hot…and bothered.

Based on the 'You like what you see?' expression on his face, again, he knew exactly what she'd been thinking. The man was too cocky for his own good.

Krissy tilted her head down and pretended to look for something on the desk in front of her. "Stupid pregnancy hormones would have me doing the deed with the devil himself just to get some satisfaction." Good thing Krissy had more self-control than that.

"So I'm the devil?" Spencer asked, standing right in front of her, with a way too amused smile on his nauseatingly handsome face. He handed her a folder.

Krissy took it. "You weren't supposed to hear that." Heck, she hadn't even realized she'd said the words out loud. "I blame pregnancy brain."

The look he gave her screamed, "You're a total nut job," although without words.

Maybe she was. "It's a real thing. Look it up. It's like a pregnant woman's body is so busy growing another human being, the brain gets overloaded and doesn't filter stuff that shouldn't come out of her mouth or remember stuff she's supposed to do. It doesn't comprehend the same or think the same. I hope it goes back to working normally once all this is over."

His smile made her insides feel all fluttery.

Then he opened his mouth. "Your brain never worked normally."

"Careful," she gave him the stink eye. "Or I'll call Kira and tell her you're upsetting me. She's gotten even more overprotective now that I'm pregnant." And more bossy and more opinionated and more of a pain in the butt—who Krissy loved dearly, but still a pain in the butt, which was why Krissy needed to find the energy to go apartment hunting.

"Hmmm," Spencer said. "It's not like you to let Kira fight your battles. You going to blame that on pregnancy brain too?"

"No. I'm going to blame that on mother-pro-tecting-the-health-of-her-unborn-baby brain. Stop trying to upset me, Spencer. What do you want?"

He had the good sense to look contrite. "You're right. I'm sorry." He leaned in and added, "And I'm sorry about the other day. When I told you—"

"Don't." She held up her hand to get him to stop talking. "You already apologized." About ten times in ten different messages on her cell phone. "I don't want to talk about it." Or think about it. "So if that's the only reason you're here, you can take your friend and leave now."

He looked at the man standing beside him. "This is Alfonso Gianelli, a newly acquired player with NYC United. He just arrived from Italy. I spoke with Derrick and then Kira yesterday. She said she could get him in for a full physical this morn-ing. We'd like him to be able to start practicing with the team as soon as possible."

Nice of her darling sister not to mention a word about it. Krissy held out her hand. "Nice to meet you."

Alfonso smiled a charming smile, brought her hand to his lips and kissed her knuckles.

Spencer flashed him an annoyed look and said

something in what sounded like Italian. Alfonso dropped her hand.

Killjoy.

"He doesn't speak much English," Spencer said.

Krissy looked Alfonso over and smiled. "He doesn't need to."

"Is Kira here?"

"She's in the back." Krissy checked the spelling of Alfonso's name on the paperwork Spencer had given her then wrote it on the label of a specimen cup and handed it to the patient along with two antiseptic cleansing wipes. "We'll need a specimen for a basic urinalysis," she told Spencer. "Does he need a drug screen?"

"Already done."

"Bathroom's over there." Krissy pointed.

Spencer spoke to Alfonso in Italian and the other man walked toward the bathroom.

Krissy couldn't stop herself from watching him walk away, even if she wanted to, which she didn't. "That is one fine backside on that man." Tight and round and just begging to be squeezed.

"Stop trying to make me jealous," Spencer snapped.

"I'm not trying to make you jealous." For that

to happen he'd have to care about her, even the tiniest bit, which he didn't. "I'm merely stating my opinion." If verbalizing her opinion bothered Spencer, well, bonus points for that!

"How are you feeling?" he asked.

Now he was going to be nice? Which meant she should be nice too? Fine. "I'm feeling well. No more pains. Derrick has been checking my blood pressure three times a day. Mornings and afternoons it's been running around one hundred and thirty-eight systolic, seventy-four diastolic. In the evenings it's been spiking a bit. But I think that's because by the evening time I've taken all I can handle of Kira commenting on everything I do and eat and telling me what I should be doing and eating." She lowered her voice and looked him straight in the eye when she added, "While I know she loves me and just wants what's best for me, she is absolutely driving me crazy, more crazy than you drive me, which is something I'd never thought possible. If I don't find an apartment soon there's a good chance I might wind up back in the hospital strapped to a bed in an isolation room for the rest of my pregnancy."

And he was smiling again. Frustrating man.

"You find something amusing about me being strapped to a bed in an isolation room for the rest of my pregnancy?"

His smile grew. He didn't even try to hide it. "I find *you* amusing, Krissy. Always have."

She looked away. "Not always."

A woman carrying a small child walked in and got in line behind Spencer. Krissy leaned to the side to see her. "May I help you?" She needed a little break from the soon-to-be godfather of her baby.

Spencer stepped away, far enough to respect the woman's privacy while Krissy checked her in. "You're all set." Krissy gave the woman a friendly smile as she handed back her insurance card. "A nurse will be with you in a few minutes."

No sooner had the woman left to find a seat in the waiting room, Alfonso returned. Perfect timing. Krissy held out a little plastic tray and he set his urine specimen on it. Then she placed their new patient paperwork on a clipboard, hooked on a pen, and handed it to Spencer. "Do the best you can to help him fill this out. When you're done, I'll take you back."

While Spencer and Alfonso took two chairs in

the waiting room, Krissy accessed the computer system to see if Kira had already set up a new patient file for Alfonso. Of course her ever efficient sister had. Then she walked Alfonso's urine specimen back to their small lab, slid on a pair of latex gloves, and completed a dipstick urinalysis. After waiting the required length of time, she loaded the normal results into the computer on the counter.

"Hey," Kira said from behind her. "Why aren't you out at the desk?"

Krissy turned around to face her. "Why didn't you warn me Spencer was coming in today?"

Kira walked over to grab the phlebotomy tray. "Because I didn't know *he'd* be here. He called the answering service over the weekend. They've been having problems getting immediate appointments with the general practitioner they'd been using. He asked if we could complete a physical exam on a new player today. He said someone on the athletic training staff would be bringing him over." She handed the phlebotomy tray to Krissy. "Since you're here, I need blood drawn in room three. Orders are here." Kira handed Krissy her laptop. "I'll go get started on the physical exam for Spencer's soccer player."

"No need." Krissy stood. "I'll do it."

"You sure you feel up to it?" Kira studied her. "When I say feel up to it, I mean mentally and emotionally. He had you pretty upset the other day."

"If Spencer is going to be a part of my baby's life, I need to learn how to deal with him." She walked toward the door. "Best I do it in a medical setting where there's resuscitative equipment available."

After drawing five tubes of blood from a middle-aged female and packaging them to be picked up for processing, Krissy freshened the paper liner on the exam table in room nine then returned to the waiting room. "Alfonso Gianelli," she called out.

Alfonso smiled and stood. Spencer stood, too. When the men approached, Krissy said to Alfonso, "Are you okay with him going in with you?"

Alfonso looked at Spencer who said something in Italian.

Alfonso turned back to Krissy and said, "Yes."

Krissy looked up at Spencer. "How do I know what he's saying 'yes' to?"

"I'm here to translate," Spencer said. "Word for word." He walked past her. "Where do you want us?"

Krissy walked them back to the scale and took Alfonso's height and weight. Then, with his back to the eye chart—because Krissy didn't trust him not to cheat—Spencer helped translate Alfonso's letters for the eye exam. After that Krissy walked them to the exam room where she completed a hearing exam and took Alfonso's temperature, pulse, respirations, and blood pressure. Spencer watched every move she made.

After going through the physical exam health screening questions—with Spencer's help—and entering all of the information into her laptop, Krissy took an exam gown from the drawer and handed it to Alfonso. "Please tell him to take everything off. The gown opens in the back."

No sooner had she escaped to the hallway, Spencer caught up with her. "Hey," he said, gently taking her by the arm. "Is there someplace we can talk in private?"

"I'm working." Krissy tried to pull away.

He released her. "I know. So am I. It'll only take a few minutes."

Fine. Krissy switched the plastic markers to the right of the door to red, indicating the patient was ready to be seen by the doctor. Then she led Spencer into the staff lunchroom. Once inside she closed the door, picked up the receiver on the wall-mounted phone, and called the front desk. "I'm taking a break in the lunchroom if anyone needs me."

After hanging up, she crossed her arms over her large belly and turned to look at Spencer. "You have two minutes." She glanced at the clock on the microwave. "Go."

He reached into the front pocket of his slacks and took out a folded up sheet of paper. "I know you're supposed to be resting. Which I hope you're doing?"

Since he looked more concerned than confrontational, she told him, "I am. And I'm taking it easy at work, too. Believe me, Kira makes sure of it."

"Good. Figuring you might be too tired to do it yourself, I did some research," he held up the paper. "From what I've read, a woman in her third trimester of pregnancy, which you're in, should take Lamaze classes to learn how to breathe and cope with contractions, even if she's thinking of getting an epidural."

Wow. Of all the words that could have come out of Spencer Penn's mouth at that moment, Krissy never would have expected to hear 'Lamaze classes' and 'epidural' tossed into a conversation.

When she didn't respond, because, wow, she was still trying to process what'd just happened, Spencer kept right on talking. "This is a list of local hospitals and their birthing classes, everything from baby care to breastfeeding."

Krissy fought back a smile. Did Spencer Penn really just say the word breastfeeding? This entire encounter could only be described as bizarre.

Either he didn't pick up on her amusement or he didn't care. "Your doctor's office probably gives Lamaze classes, most do. You should find out about that when you go for your first appointment there. Is Kira going to be your coach?"

"My coach?"

"Come on, Krissy. You're killing me."

He rubbed his hand over his head and Krissy wondered if his hair was as soft as it looked. Jeez. Where the heck had that come from? She shook her head to clear her wayward thoughts and get back on topic.

"Haven't you thought about who's going to be in the delivery room with you?"

No, she hadn't. In fact, she purposely worked very hard to occupy her mind so she didn't have to think about it, which was getting tougher and tougher as her delivery date approached. Of course Kira would do it if she asked, but her sister already had so many responsibilities. Too many responsibilities. Yet the thought of going through it alone…she looked away from him through the window to the parking lot outside so he couldn't see her fear. "Boy, you're taking this godfather stuff pretty seriously. I'd kind of figured your re-sponsibilities wouldn't start until after the baby is born. So you can relax." And back off. Unless… she swung back around. "Unless you don't trust me to do what's best for my baby." That had to be it. "Unless you don't think I'm capable of man-aging—"

"Whoa." He held up both hands. "Calm down. I'm not here to upset you, I'm trying to help."

"Well I don't need your help. And I don't need Kira's help. I'm going to do this on my own. I *can* do it on my own. I *will* do it on my own." She repeated her mantra of late.

"But you don't have to do it on your own, Krissy. Jarrod wouldn't want you to go through all of this on your own."

Jarrod. God how she missed him, how she wished he was here. Tears pricked her eyes.

"Let me help you."

"Why would you want to help me?" she snapped. "You blame me for Jarrod's death." Now *she* blamed herself, too. "You hate me."

"I don't hate you."

Even though he towered over her, Krissy stared him down. "Liar."

"I don't. I know you're not responsible for Jarrod's death. He was an adult. He made his own decisions, however misguided they may have been. I'm sorry for what I said and how I acted when you came to my apartment. I was mean. You didn't deserve it. Seems I had some unresolved issues where Jarrod's death was concerned. But I'm over them now." He motioned to a chair. "Please, sit down. You look ready to collapse."

Now that he mentioned it, she kind of felt ready to collapse, too. Probably because this was the most energy she'd exerted since she'd left the hospital three days ago. So she sat.

Spencer sat, too.

"Glad I was available to help you resolve your issues," Krissy said, even if, as a result, she now felt even more weighted down by guilt. "Happy to be of service." In truth she wasn't happy at all. Rather than look at him, Krissy reached to take a packet of artificial sweetener from the basket in the center of the table and started flipping it between her fingers.

"Hey." Spencer reached over, slid a knuckle under her chin, and tilted her face up so she had to look at him. "I'm sorry, truly sorry, from the bottom of my cold, unfeeling heart," he said, with such sincerity she believed him. But the damage was done, the truth had come out—about Jarrod and about what Spencer really thought of her—and there'd be no unhearing it.

Only moving her eyes, Krissy glanced at the clock on the microwave. "You've exceeded your two minutes." She didn't like this nice, self-deprecating version of Spencer, didn't like the way it made her feel, didn't know how to respond to it.

Spencer released her chin and held out his hand. "Can we have a truce? Maybe start fresh?"

"Why?"

He reached down to her lap and took her hand into his. "We were friends once, good friends for a long time."

But they weren't friends anymore.

"And that's my best friend's baby in there." He pointed to her belly. "Can't we put our differences aside and do what's best for Jarrod's baby?"

Rather than remind him that little J.J. was part her baby too, Krissy thought about his proposal. She'd spent most of the last five and a half years traveling from place to place and had no local friends, as in good friends she'd feel comfortable calling for help in the middle of the night, in White Plains, where she now lived to be close to her sister. It'd be nice to know, in case of emergency, she had someone she could call aside from Kira and Derrick.

"Come on," Spencer said with a handsome smile. He let go of her hand and held his out. "Friends?"

After a brief hesitation, more to make him wait than anything else, Krissy shook it. "Friends."

"Good." Spencer unfolded the paper he'd set down on the table and turned it so she could read what he'd written.

"On top," he pointed, "is the hospital information. Down here," he moved his finger lower, "is the rental agent for my building."

"Whoa." Krissy sat back. "No."

"It's not my intent to overstep, but you mentioned you needed an apartment."

"I am not moving into your building."

He looked offended. "Why not? It's nice. It has security. It has ample parking and is close to shopping, Derrick's office, and White Plains Hospital. Also, I checked, they have two one bedroom units and three two bedroom units available for immediate occupancy. With a recommendation from me, you could probably be in by the end of this week, early next, assuming your credit's okay."

While Krissy liked the sound of 'immediate occupancy', "I can't afford it."

"I happen to know you were the sole beneficiary of a huge life insurance policy. You couldn't possibly have…" He hesitated, his eyes studying her face as he seemed to be trying to figure out the safest way to finish his statement.

Krissy stared back, at a crossroad. She could pounce on him for even thinking she'd blow through all the money Jarrod had left her. Or she could avoid confrontation and take the high road, so to speak, which is what she decided to do. After all, Spencer was trying to be nice. She could try too. "I have every cent Jarrod left me, and it's been accruing interest for the past five years."

Spencer let out a relieved breath. "Good. Then you can afford—"

"No I can't. I need someplace cheap. What if my baby is a genius and wants to go to an Ivy League college? I want to be able to send him. Then there's graduate school or medical school."

Spencer smiled. "Getting a little ahead of yourself there, aren't you? The baby's not even born yet and you're planning his college education?"

"No. I'm being a responsible parent and trying to ensure the best future I can give my and Jarrod's son."

Spencer simply stared at her with an odd look on his face.

"What?"

"Nothing," he answered, glancing away. "I just…didn't…"

Krissy finished for him, "Expect I'd want to be a good, responsible parent?" She could have gotten offended. Instead she looked down at her belly and rubbed each side. "Jarrod entrusted me with a part of him. He believed in me, believed I'd make a good mother for his child. I'm honored to have his baby, to give his parents a grandson. I loved him, maybe not the same way he loved me," she wiped at a tear threatening to spill out of her right eye, "but I did love him. And I love our baby and will do everything in my power to see he grows up happy and healthy and is afforded every opportunity I can give him."

She lifted her eyes to Spencer. "I'm not the same person I was in high school. I may not do things according to everyone else's schedule, but I do what needs to be done by the time it needs to be done."

She pushed back from the table and stood. "Thank you for this information." She picked the paper up from the table, folded it, and slid it into the pocket of her scrub top.

Spencer stood, too. "I picked my apartment building, because I'm there. Well, not all the time. It's soccer season now, so I'm busier than during off season. I rotate traveling to away games with another assistant athletic trainer." He slid his hands into the front pockets in his slacks, the move relaxed and confident and oh, so sexy. "What I'm trying to say is, I thought it would be nice for you to have a friend close by just in case. Middle of the night? I can hop on the elevator, be there in minutes, rather than getting into the car and driving to wherever you are. Unless there's some other guy you'd rather call, then by all means, call him. Either way, I don't plan on bothering you."

"Or checking up on me?" Like Kira tended to do.

"Not up, but checking *in* on you, to make sure you're okay, to see if you need anything." He held up both hands. "That's all. I promise to respect your privacy. And I won't ever come over without being invited."

Maybe that'd work, if the rents were reasonable, and until she figured out what she wanted to do and where she wanted to be long term, after J.J.'s birth. Maybe she'd move back to New York City to be closer to Jarrod's parents. "Thank you, Spencer. Really." She looked up into his eyes. "For the record, no, there is no other guy I'd rather call. Well, except for Derrick, but then Kira would come too, and I'm trying to avoid bothering her. And, yes. I'll think about looking into available apartments in your building."

Someone knocked on the door.

As Krissy went to answer it Spencer said, "Great. And if you need a Lamaze coach…"

"Absolutely not."

CHAPTER FOUR

FIVE DAYS LATER, on Saturday morning, Spencer found himself driving to Lamaze class with an unhappy Krissy in the front passenger seat of his car.

"How do you like your new place?" he asked, trying to make conversation.

"It's fine," she answered, sounding bored, as she looked out the window.

Much better than fine, her one-bedroom apartment in his building—because the rent on the one-bedroom was less than the rent on the two-bedroom—was beautiful. Spacious, with freshly painted walls, refurbished hardwood floors and an updated kitchen. He knew the details for certain, because he'd helped Derrick and Kira move her in on Thursday night, not that she'd required much help since all she'd brought with her were two duffle bags, five or six boxes, and a small, twin-size bed.

Now, every time he rode the elevator past the fourth floor, to or from his apartment on the sixth floor, he thought about her, wondered if she was okay, if she needed anything.

Yes, as she'd pointed out during their chat in the staff lunchroom at Derrick's office, Jarrod had entrusted her with a part of himself. Well, Jarrod had also entrusted Spencer to look after and help the woman he'd loved completely and the child he'd entrusted her with. Spencer took his responsibilities very seriously, always had. Jarrod knew that, had seen Spencer step up after his father had died, keeping a close eye on his younger sisters, protecting and guiding them, like his father would have. Better than his father would have.

As much as Spencer had been looking forward to his newfound freedom from his mother and sisters, the truth was he'd been feeling a little lost for the past few months. No way he wanted to take on the responsibility of another woman in his life, one mother and two sisters were enough, thank you very much. But the more he thought about it, the more the idea of helping and looking after Krissy and her baby, at least for now, until they were both settled, started to grow on him. It gave him a purpose, made him feel needed again. And just like researching future occupations, scholarships and colleges with his sisters, and helping his mom figure out college loans and investment strategies for retirement planning, Spencer had put in the hours to research pregnancy, labor and delivery, and caring for a newborn.

The timing worked.

During soccer season he could be around for Krissy, help her out. After she had the baby he could stop in here and there, make sure little J.J. was well cared for. Then, at the end of soccer season, he'd take off for a few weeks of rest and relaxation.

Playing the role of godfather to Krissy and Jarrod's baby didn't have to ruin his plans.

"I really appreciate you coming with me today," Krissy said, again, for the… Spencer had lost track of how many times she'd said it. "I have lots of friends down in New York City. But Kira moved herself and my mom up to White Plains while I was out in Hawaii. I don't know many people here yet."

She repositioned herself in her seat, again, either uncomfortable or antsy. He couldn't tell which.

"No problem," he answered, again, like he'd answered each time she'd stated her appreciation. The crash course version of Lamaze—three hours on Saturday morning and three hours on Sunday afternoon—worked out perfectly with his work schedule. Luckily he hadn't been scheduled to travel to Canada with the team. Only a few injured players had stayed behind for rehab so he could easily flex his schedule.

"Kira had to work today. I'm sure if I'd asked, she would have come tomorrow."

"But I insisted on going both days because—"

"Attending only half of the class won't make either one of you a proficient coach," she finished. "That makes sense. If you're even around when I go into labor."

"I'll be around."

"What if you're traveling with the team?"

He wouldn't be. Come Monday he'd be talking to management about his need to stay local for the next few weeks. "Even when the team is out of town, one assistant athletic trainer stays behind to work with the players who are injured. And not all of the guys travel with the team. The ones who remain here still practice, so an athletic trainer needs to be on site."

"Don't go changing your schedule at work because of me. I mean it's not like I *need* a coach." She continued to stare out the window as Spencer pulled into the parking lot behind her doctor's office. "I mean I *am* a nurse. I *did* do a labor and delivery rotation as a nursing student. I *know* what Lamaze is."

She demonstrated a breathing sequence he recognized from the Lamaze research he'd done online to prepare for the class. "During which phase of labor are you supposed to use that particular breathing technique?"

Still looking out the window, she crossed her arms over her chest, defiant, and said, "When it hurts, that's when."

Spencer pulled into a vacant spot, turned off the car, and removed his seat belt. Then he shifted in his seat to face her. "What's the matter?"

"Nothing's the matter." She wouldn't look at him.

"You're all sulky."

That got a rise out of her and she swung around to face him. "I am *not* all sulky."

Oh, yes, she was. It's not like he'd never seen her sulky before. This was her standard MO back in high school, every time he and/or Jarrod had tried to get her to do something she didn't want to do—like go to geometry class, stay after school for extra help in U.S. History, or walk directly home with them rather than getting into trouble with the kids who hung out at the deli on the corner.

In the past he'd have made a joke or poked fun to get her riled up. But not today. Today was too important. "What's wrong, Krissy?"

She turned back to the window. "I don't want to be here."

Now they were getting somewhere. "Why not?"

Shoulders hunched, she shrugged and mumbled something.

"What?"

"I'm not ready," she said quietly. "For the whole giving birth thing."

"You're not ready? I've got news for you. This baby's going to be coming in the next couple of weeks whether you're ready or not so you'd better get yourself ready."

She turned on him. "Don't be mean to me, Spencer. I really can't handle you being mean to me right now." Her voice sounded like she might be on the verge of tears as she turned to look down at her hands fidgeting in her lap.

A moment of vulnerability from the tough-talking, fiercely independent and confident Krissy took him by surprise.

"I didn't think this whole 'have Jarrod's baby' idea through carefully enough," she went on. "The pregnancy itself? Not totally awful. Raising little J.J.?" She caressed her belly lovingly. "I'm sure I'll get the hang of it."

Get the hang of it?

Her eyes met his again. "It's the getting the baby from in here," she pointed to her belly, "out into the world that's giving me some trouble."

"Krissy—"

"I have four weeks left until my due date," she cut him off. "In four weeks I'll have to be ready and I will be ready. Until then I don't want to talk about it or think about it or worry about it."

He reached for her hand, finding it ice cold. Whoa. "Hey." He gave it a squeeze. "You know it's normal to be scared." For sure he would be. "But women have been having babies for centuries, a lot of them over and over again. It's a very natural process."

"Says a man who has never experienced and will never have to experience the act of pushing a fifteen pound baby out of an opening the size of a walnut."

Smiling probably wasn't the best response, but he smiled anyway. "You're not having a fifteen pound baby."

She slid him a look. "You don't know that."

That's right. He didn't, at least not for sure. But according to his research, the average birth weight for babies was seven and a half pounds, with a range of five and a half pounds on the low end of normal and ten pounds on the high end. Since, even pregnant, Krissy was on the small side, he'd guess her baby would be on the small side too.

"All this talk about individualized birth plans and creating the experience you want. A bunch of bull." She waved off the idea. "I told my doctor I wanted the unconscious plan. A scheduled cesarean, so I know when J.J. is coming. General anesthesia, so I can sleep through the painful parts and wake up relaxed and happy and ready to get started on the mother son bonding."

She may be scared, but she managed to be amusing at the same time. "General anesthesia, that's your birth plan." She had to be kidding. Although she didn't look like she was kidding at all.

"Don't judge me, Spencer. I don't like pain. Pain hurts. And to have to endure it for hours and hours and maybe days." She wrapped her arms around herself and shivered. Then she shook her head. "Nuh-uh. Not for me."

"How'd your doctor respond to your request for general anesthesia?"

"He laughed." She looked like she couldn't believe he'd had the nerve. "Like I was joking around. Well I wasn't. I was totally serious." She fidgeted with her necklace. "Then he told the nurse to sign me up for the next Lamaze class. I told him I wasn't available this weekend but he told me to make myself available that he expected me to be here and would be very disappointed if I didn't show up. Like a parent tells a child. 'I'll be very disappointed if you don't show up,'" she mimicked in a deep, authoritative voice. Then she turned to look out the window. "I really don't want to disappoint him but…maybe I should find a new doctor."

"You don't need a new doctor." Spencer liked the guy, especially since he seemed to know how to handle patients like Krissy. "Maybe he wanted you to take this weekend's class because he thinks you're going to deliver early."

Krissy's eyes went wide and all the color drained from her face. "Don't say that. Don't even think it."

"Lamaze is supposed to teach you how to cope with the discomfort of contractions," Spencer said, keeping his voice calm. "Give the class a chance. Maybe you'll learn something. Maybe it'll alleviate some of your fears."

"I doubt that."

He gave her hand a shake. "I promise to take you for a hot fudge sundae when it's all over." Her favorite, at least it used to be.

"No." She shook her head and pulled her hand from his. "I've made up my mind. If my current OB-GYN won't knock me out with medication, I'm going to find one who will. So all this Lamaze stuff is going to be a total waste of time that could be much better spent shopping for furniture and baby stuff."

"As a nurse you know natural childbirth is best for the baby."

She turned to look at him, or, more specifically, to stare down at his crotch. "Hmmm. What do you think we could do to you to simulate what natural childbirth might feel like?" She smiled sweetly. "Then we can talk about natural childbirth."

Okay. Not going there.

"I have seen women give birth," she said. "I have listened to their screams on the Labor and Delivery floor. I have actually witnessed the birthing process, live and in person. I can tell you, in no uncertain terms, nothing short of knowing I will be heavily medicated so I can sleep through delivery, will put my mind at ease."

"Krissy," he cautioned.

"What?" she snapped.

Good lord. The woman was stubborn to the end. "We're going to Lamaze class," he told her calmly. Even if he had to drag her. "Just give it a try. That's all I ask. If you hate it and find it not at all helpful, we'll leave." Not before he did his absolute best to convince her to stay. Hopefully once he got her inside she'd calm down.

"You're not going to leave me alone about this, are you?"

He shook his head. No. He wasn't.

"Fine." She threw open the door. "Let's go waste the next three hours of our lives. Time we will never get back, by the way." She slammed the door shut behind her.

Spencer didn't care. She'd gotten out of the car, and that's all that mattered. Reaching into the backseat, he grabbed his pad and pen and the two pillows Krissy had brought, then he climbed out, too.

One look at what he held in his hands and Krissy slammed her hands on her hips. "Really? A pad and pen? You plan to take notes?"

Just to get a rise out of her he said, "I plan to study them, too."

"Poindexter." She turned to walk up the sidewalk. "Some things never change."

He smiled as he followed, hadn't been called that name in years and he liked hearing it, especially in Krissy's annoyed voice. Just like old times. "Call me what you will, but when you're ready to give birth, I'll be ready to coach you through it."

"I plan to be *sleeping* through it." She glanced back. "But thanks."

Two hours later, in a large, dimly lit room, with Krissy laying on her side on a mat with a pillow under her head and one between her legs, Spencer, and the couples around them, got an earful of how Krissy likely sounded and acted during sex.

Vocal—gratifyingly so, a total ego boost. He dug his thumbs into her low back.

"That feels sooooo good," she moaned.

Demanding—better to know than to have to guess and hope you get it right.

"Lower. Right there. Harder." She let out a deep satisfied breath. "Don't stop."

An active participant—the very best kind of bed partner.

She rolled her hips and arched her back. "Up a little. No, down."

He slid his hands up, then down, following her directions.

After her "Aaahhh," accompanied by a pleasure-filled exhalation, Spencer actually found himself getting a little aroused by it all.

The teacher, a tall, slender, middle-aged woman

wearing a lab coat over street clothes, said, "Okay, time to change positions."

"Nooooo," Krissy whined loudly. "I like this position."

The teacher smiled at Spencer. "Looks like someone has the magic touch."

Why thank you, thank you very much.

Krissy turned onto her back. "Don't look so proud of yourself." She whacked him in the face with the pillow that'd been between her knees. "It's only because I haven't...been touched...in a long time."

The teacher called out, "Next position I want my partners to take a seat on the floor, backs straight, legs opened, knees bent."

Shoot, just when things were starting to get interesting.

The teacher continued, "Now I want my mamas to sit between their partner's legs, back to their chests, and rest your head on their shoulder."

Krissy maneuvered into position.

"Partners," the teacher said. "Slide your arms under and around," she demonstrated on another couple, "then clasp your fingers together on the top of her belly."

Spencer did as instructed.

Krissy felt so good and smelled so good. Her soft, fragrant hair tickled his cheek. Her body heated his wherever they touched, which felt like everywhere. How many times had his teenage self dreamed of holding her this close?

She wiggled her bottom then stiffened.

Krissy may have been clueless about Jarrod's true feelings for her, but she didn't miss the key indicator of how Spencer was feeling about her at that particular moment.

She wiggled her bottom against his arousal again then turned her head close to his ear and whispered, "Really, Spencer? I'm big as a manatee and we're at Lamaze class of all places."

She wasn't big as a manatee. She was full and lush and even sexier than she'd been in high school. "Sorry," he said. Thinking fast he added, "It's only because I haven't…been touched…in a long time."

Krissy pinched his thigh.

He tried to muffle his laugh in the side of her neck.

Then she wiggled against him again.

The minx probably planned to torture him for

the rest of the class. Well, no way he'd allow that. Determined to put a stop to it, Spencer leaned in close, moved his mouth to her ear and quietly warned, "Don't start something you can't finish."

Krissy stiffened.

Then she pulled his head down and whispered back, "Oh, I can finish, Spencer, in so many different ways. FYI, those rumors back in high school were true." She licked his ear. "I give an amazing blow job."

Lord help him.

A rookie mistake. He should have known Krissy would take his words as a challenge and use her confident sexuality to say something outrageous that would give her the upper hand.

It'd worked, too. The image of a naked Krissy, on her knees at his feet, looking up at him as she took his erection into her hot, wet mouth filled his mind. At the anticipated feel of her sucking him deep into the back of her throat, over and over, he grew bigger, and harder, and more aroused.

She slid her backside in even closer, readjusting her position again, rubbing from side to side against him until all Spencer could think about was lifting her onto his lap, lowering her leggings and his zipper, and entering her from behind, thrusting up into her, again and again until…

This had to stop.

Spencer wasn't a sexually inexperienced teenager anymore. He was a man who liked to take charge and be in control.

So he called her bluff, leaning down to whisper, "Maybe I didn't get much action back in high school, but I've made up for it in adulthood." Not really, but what he lacked in quantity he'd made up for in quality. "You're not the only one with amazing talent. In fact, if you can keep quiet, I bet I can get you off in minutes, right here, right now, in this room full of people, without anyone knowing."

There. Take that! And just to give his words some added oomph, he ran his tongue around the rim of her ear eliciting a small but most rewarding tremble from her.

Krissy let out a breath and melted into him.

"What do you say?" He took things one step further, moving one of the pillows partially into her lap to hide what he was about to do from those around them. Then he slid his hand up her inner thigh, slowly, waiting for her to stop him, knowing she would.

"Krissy and Spencer," the instructor called out in an unpleasant, disciplinary voice, her eyes focused in on the pillow between Krissy's legs as if she could tell what he was doing underneath it.

Busted!

"Sorry," Spencer said. "Krissy had an itch she couldn't reach."

Based on her expression, the instructor wasn't buying it.

"I'm sorry, too," Krissy said, repositioning herself, again, in a move that made it perfectly clear to Spencer that she wasn't sorry at all. "Spencer had a question about your diagram. I was trying to answer it as best I could."

The instructor turned back to her oversize poster of the female genitalia. "Would you like to share your question with the class?" she asked Spencer.

"No." Spencer shook his head, feeling his face heat.

A few of the men in the room laughed.

"Okay, then," the teacher said. "As I was saying…"

With the attention no longer on them, Krissy

whispered, "Just like high school, you're always getting me into trouble."

It was all Spencer could do not to laugh out loud. Invoking quite a bit of self-control to keep his indignation from showing, he whispered, "*Me* getting *you* into trouble? I don't think so! Not then and not now. You and your moaning." He moved in close to her ear to mimic, "'That feels soooooo good.'"

She gave him a tiny elbow to the ribs. "Well I'm sorry for moaning. I promise to be quiet from now on."

He didn't want her sorry and he didn't want her quiet. He wanted her as aroused and off-kilter as he was feeling. So he pressed his mouth to her ear and told her, "Never apologize for moaning when I make you feel good. I like making women moan in pleasure, means I have them right where I want them."

Krissy pinched his thigh. A lot harder that time.

Ouch! He resisted the urge to rub it.

"Pay attention," she snapped. "You're the reason we're here."

Right. Lamaze class. Birth coach. Huge responsibility.

Spencer needed every bit of willpower, determination and concentration in his possession to ignore the sensual woman between his legs and turn his attention back to Lamaze class. But he did it. Thank goodness the class ended twenty-five minutes later.

CHAPTER FIVE

KRISSY CAME AWAKE to someone knocking on the door to her apartment, but was too exhausted to get up from the couch to answer it. When the knocking stopped, she closed her eyes and started to sink back into sleep.

Until her cell phone rang.

She picked it up from the coffee table. Seeing Spencer's name and number on the screen she accepted the call. "Sorry. I completely forgot you were planning to stop by. Did you win?" His soccer team had played a Saturday afternoon game.

"Yeah. Three to one. Where are you?" he asked. "Your car's parked in your spot but you're not answering your door."

"Because I'm sleeping." She stretched. "At least I was sleeping until *someone* started knocking on my door."

"Open up," he said. "I have a surprise for you."

She wanted to, really she did. Even though he'd

made it a point to call her every night around eight o'clock—a call she'd started to look forward to—due to their busy schedules, she hadn't seen him in almost a week, since Sunday's Lamaze class. But as much as she'd like to show off her handiwork in putting together J.J.'s crib all by herself, she just couldn't muster the energy to walk to the door. "Come back later."

"It's ice cream," he sing-songed.

Krissy's stomach growled. "What kind of ice cream?" No way she'd put forth the monumental effort to heft her massive body off of the couch for anything less than a hot fudge sundae or banana split.

"A hot fudge sundae, just like I promised."

After all the sexual back and forth during Lamaze class on Saturday, Spencer had gone quiet, making things feel weird between them. So Krissy had claimed she needed a nap and asked for a rain check on the ice cream, eager to put a little distance between them. On Sunday, Spencer didn't have time for ice cream because he had to head straight to work—after dropping her back home—for some late treatments.

Krissy's mouth started to water. "Give me a

sec." She rolled onto her side and hauled herself into a sitting position, her arms and upper body feeling almost too heavy to lift. *Hot fudge sundae.* She set her hands on her knees, leaned forward and pushed up.

When she opened the door Spencer said, "You look exhausted."

"I *am* exhausted." Down to her bones. Too exhausted to remain upright, so Krissy turned around and headed back to the couch. "Which is why I was sleeping." She sat then lied down on her side and closed her eyes again. "Put the ice cream in the freezer, will you? I'll eat it later. Thank you."

"Are you feeling okay?"

She appreciated the concern in his voice. "Just a very busy week catching up with me." Tippy, Mom's caregiver over at Kira's house, hadn't been feeling well so Krissy had been helping out over there in the evenings after work so Kira could spend some alone time with Derrick before she went down to spend the night. "Today I worked until three in the afternoon then I came home did some laundry, cleaned the bathroom and got involved in putting J.J.'s crib together." What a nightmare that had been.

She heard Spencer open her freezer. "I told you I'd put the crib together."

"And *I* told *you* I could do it myself."

"You know it's okay to let people help you."

"I know." But since the age of fourteen, since Mom's brain injury, Krissy had gotten used to doing things for herself. With her father no longer a part of their family, an eighteen-year-old Kira had been stretched thin, going to college while managing the expenses, the condo, and Mom's care. Krissy tried hard not to be an additional burden, to anyone, even though Kira might tell a different tale.

She heard Spencer walk into the living room. Something rattled. "Looks nice. But what's with that pile of screws and springs on the floor?"

Krissy yawned. "They were left over after I finished."

Spencer let out a breath.

Krissy didn't have the energy to read into it and start a fight.

"Have you eaten dinner?" he asked.

"I will when I wake up." Krissy yawned again,

thankful Spencer had stopped talking, thankful for the quiet, thankful to be able to go back… to…sleep…

Sometime later Krissy opened her eyes to darkness and the smell of—she inhaled to be sure—Chinese stir-fry chicken. Hunger made her empty stomach ache. She turned to see the light on in her kitchen and someone moving around in there. "Spencer?" Who else could it be?

"Hey," he said, coming to stand in the doorway. "You're awake. I thought I was going to have to eat without you."

"What time is it?" Krissy sat up.

"Almost eight-thirty." Spencer walked into the living room and held out his hand.

Krissy latched on to it and he pulled her up. "Thank you."

He bowed at the waist then motioned to the kitchen. "Dinner is served."

As much as she wanted to eat, "Bathroom first." She hurried down the hall. One glance in the mirror and, "My God!" A wild woman looked back at her. Hair matted on one side, sticking out in all directions on the other. Eye makeup smudged.

And drool, she wiped her mouth. Thank goodness the living room had been dark.

How she looked shouldn't matter. It was only Spencer, after all. But for some reason it did matter. He always managed to look good and she wanted to look good too. So after she emptied her overfull bladder, she took a few minutes to freshen up.

In the kitchen Spencer greeted her with a smile. "Feel better?"

She smiled back, feeling uncharacteristically shy. "Yes. Much." He'd been busy while she was sleeping. "Wow. You went all out." The table neatly set, all the pots washed and in the drain board, a yummy looking chicken stir fry with vegetables beautifully plated over brown rice and ready to be eaten. "I know for sure I didn't have broccoli or red peppers," she pointed out.

He pulled out a chair. "You had chicken breast, carrots and soy sauce. I combined that with some stuff I had and voilà!" He motioned to the serving dish. "A healthy dinner for two and two-thirds."

She smiled again at him referring to J.J. as two-thirds.

"We make a good team," he added as he sat beside her.

They'd made a good team at Lamaze class, too. "I'm impressed." She inhaled deeply. "I hope it tastes as good as it looks."

"It does." He served them both.

So confident. Wait a minute. "Let me guess. Cooking classes?"

He wouldn't look at her. "It was something to do."

"Good place to pick up women?" she teased.

"Good place to learn to make healthy food taste good," he countered. "Now eat." He pointed to her plate with his fork. "Before it gets cold."

Typical Spencer. Always learning, always taking classes or workshops to be the best he could be. As she enjoyed her first delicious mouthful, Krissy was glad he hadn't changed in that regard. "It's fantastic. You can cook for me anytime."

"I like your new table and chairs."

Of course he did, since he's the one who'd made her get them, even though she'd insisted she didn't need them because she mostly ate on the couch in front of the television...that is, when she ate at home, which she'd likely be doing much more of once she had little J.J.

"Good thing you have them so we can have this nice dinner together," he said. "And they fit perfectly in your kitchen."

Just like he'd said they would.

She looked up at him. "You were right, okay? There, I said it. Happy now?"

He smiled his handsome smile and Krissy's insides warmed. "As a matter of fact, yes I am."

"...you're not the only one with amazing talent... I bet I can get you off in minutes, right here, right now, in this room full of people, without anyone knowing."

Starting the ninth month of her pregnancy, with another man's baby, and she couldn't get Spencer's words out of her head, couldn't move past the way his touch had made her feel...so alive... so needy. A tingle of intrigue buzzed around her insides, settling between her legs.

"Hey." He ducked his head to catch her line of sight. "You okay?"

Nope. Not at all. "Yup." She forced a smile and stuffed more food into her mouth so she wouldn't be expected to say anything else. While she chewed she looked at Spencer, so neatly put together in a very virile package. Then she looked around her now neat kitchen. In so many ways he reminded her of Kira, organized, prompt, smart, and loyal, a know-it-all who usually turned out to be right. It irked her a bit. But he'd been so nice over the past two weeks, she could overlook it… as long as she didn't spend too much time thinking about it. So she changed the subject to something neutral. "How was work today?"

"Busy." He took a sip of water. "I've got to go in tomorrow morning. Not too early, but for a few hours."

He'd told her that during the soccer season, more often than not, he went into work seven days a week. "How's Alfonso doing?" Maybe she'd only met the new star player of NYC United once, when she'd helped with his physical exam, but she'd seen him almost naked, which put them on first name basis, as far as she was concerned. "I saw him go in for that header at the same time as the player from the other team." She cringed. "It looked bad." He'd gone down hard and had needed to be helped off the field.

"I didn't know you were a soccer fan."

She wasn't. At least she hadn't been prior to learning of Spencer's job with NYC United. Now, whenever she could, she watched the games, hoping for a glimpse of Spencer on the sidelines, or better yet, seeing him in action on the field. Not that she'd tell *him* that. "I'm a fan of the Italian hottie, Alfonso Gianelli."

"You and hundreds of other women." Spencer sounded peeved. "He's a player, and I'm not talking about his skills with a soccer ball." He looked up from his plate. "Stay away from him."

"As if he'd have any interest in me now." Thirty pounds heavier than normal, which even before her pregnancy tended to run toward full-figured. But she appreciated the hint of something...concern, maybe jealousy in his voice.

Spencer's eyes met hers. "Knock it off. You're beautiful and sexy and you know it."

"I'm fat," came out of her mouth before she even had a chance to process what Spencer had said.

"You're pregnant. There's a difference."

Whoa. "You think I'm beautiful and sexy?" She stood to remind him what she looked like, arching her back to make her oversize belly protrude even more than usual. "Almost nine months pregnant." She tilted her head as she stared down at him. "Have you been drinking? I mean I know I don't have any booze down here, but did you toss back a few beers up at your place when you went to raid your fridge?"

His expression totally serious, Spencer said, "No, I haven't been drinking. And yes, even at almost nine months pregnant. Now stop looking for compliments and finish eating. I'm ready for my ice cream."

Oh, no. She liked this topic of conversation and wanted to spend a little more time on it. "Hmmm." She tapped her chin. "So it was me, in all my pregnant glory, who turned you on at Lamaze class?" How flattering. "You hadn't been thinking of someone else? That impressive hard-on wasn't only because you hadn't had full body contact with a woman in a while?" A topic worthy of further discussion at a later time. "It wasn't being in a room with all those hormonal pregnant women that got you going? Tell me the truth. Do you have some kind of pregnancy fetish? Is that why you were so determined to get me to go to that class?" Krissy teased.

Fork halfway up to his mouth, Spencer froze.

Then his heated gaze locked on hers. "You found my…hard-on, as you so eloquently put it, impressive?"

Out of everything she'd just said, he'd chosen that one thing to focus in on. Such a guy. "*Now* who's looking for compliments?" God Krissy had missed this, had missed Spencer and this crazy banter between them.

Oh, so casually he removed the napkin from his lap and blotted his mouth. "As a matter of fact I *was* thinking of another woman."

Way to ruin her fun.

"Or at least another time." He stood, cleared his dishes and placed them in the sink. "You were a teenage boy's wet dream." He turned to face her, leaning his hip against the counter. "The way you teased and flirted. Your body." He shook his head. "Seeing you again…it's sent me back in time. I'm sorry. It won't happen again."

What? No need to apologize. Wait a minute. "A teenage boy's wet dream? *Your* wet dream?" She couldn't believe it. "Then why…?" When she'd offered herself to him… "Why…?" Had he been so mean, so…hurtful?

"It's a long story," he said, turning around, giving her his back.

"Tell me. I've got time."

He ran the water and soaped up the sponge. "No."

She recognized the finality of that tone, knew there'd be nothing she could do to get him to talk more on that subject. At least not right now. Krissy could be patient, could wait for a better time to bring it up. She stood and walked her dishes over to the sink. "Don't want to talk about that? How about we talk about you not being touched in a while." Standing next to him, her back to the counter, she looked up. "You know, like exactly how long 'a while' has been and why?"

"Or," in the process of rinsing a glass, he turned his head to face her. "We can talk about exactly how long 'a while' has been for *you*, and why."

Nah. That would require bringing up her relationship with Zac, and how, upon learning she was pregnant, he'd refused to do anything more than hold her hand, which she had no desire to do.

"So work it is." She returned to the table, clearing Spencer's delicious entrée. "What's the final diagnosis on Alfonso? Concussion?" She took the plastic wrap from a drawer.

"You know I can't discuss my patients with you," he said.

Right. The rules of confidentiality applied to all health care professionals, not just doctors and nurses. "So what *can* you tell me?" She wrapped up the leftovers and put them in the refrigerator, kind of liking this bit of shared domesticity and having someone to talk to. "Describe a typical work day."

"First thing we do is get the water together to keep the athletes hydrated during practices and games." He continued washing the dishes while he talked. Krissy picked up a towel and started to dry. "We stock the med kits with appropriate medical supplies. Then the athletes start coming in for pre-practice or pre-game treatments consisting of modalities such as therapeutic ultrasound or electrical stimulation—for pain control or edema reduction, manual therapy, anything from stretching to spinal and/or joint mobilization. In soccer we tape a lot of ankles as a preventative measure to avoid injuries. We attend all practices and games to handle any medical emergencies."

"What types of medical emergencies have you dealt with?"

"You name it, I've probably seen it. Everything from orthopedic injuries, sprains, strains and fractures, to head injuries, to lacerations and contusions. Heat stroke, hypoglycemic shock. Cardiac emergencies like commotio cordis."

"Commotio what?"

"A disruption of the heart rhythm as a result of a strong blow to the chest directly over the heart."

"Yikes. What do you do for that?"

"Apply an AED—automated external defibrillator—as soon as possible and activate emergency medical services to get the player to the hospital. The one time I had to deal with it, the player lived. Not all of them do."

The kitchen clean and their conversation winding down, Krissy realized she'd been enjoying their visit and didn't want him to leave. "If you don't have plans tonight, would you want to hang out and watch a movie?" she asked, turning on the light in her sparsely furnished living room then retrieving the remote from the coffee table. "We could rent something On Demand." In the fully lit room, Krissy noticed the crib, or more precisely, the missing pile of leftover pieces she'd stacked beneath it. "Hey. Did you work on the crib while I was sleeping?"

"Yeah," he called from the kitchen.

"You know I had every intention of going back over the directions to see where I went wrong. I wouldn't put J.J. in an unsafe crib."

Standing in the doorway to the kitchen, wiping his hands on a towel, Spencer said, "I know you wouldn't put J.J. in an unsafe crib."

At least that was something.

"But I wanted to help and you were sleeping so I helped."

Thank goodness. Even though she had, in fact, planned to retrace her assembly steps, she wasn't looking forward to it.

"I put together the changing table too."

Krissy lifted the box to find it empty.

"I moved it into your bedroom, but I can put it anywhere you'd like."

"Thank you," she said, meaning it. "Bedroom's fine."

"I'll put the crib in there too if that's where you want it."

"I can wheel it in there."

"So ice cream and a movie?" he asked.

Sounded great to her, she clicked on the television. But when she turned around to set the remote back down on the coffee table, her eyes slid over her small couch, the only place to sit in the living room, other than the floor. A niggling worry in the back of her mind had her thinking maybe being alone with Spencer, on the same couch, wasn't such a great idea.

"What?" he asked, still able to read her better than most.

"Uh." How to explain? She pointed to the couch. "That's the only thing I have to sit on."

"So?"

She pointed back and forth between them. "There seems to be some latent sexual chemistry between us that's, I don't know, come back to life or something."

He crossed his arms over his chest and leaned against the doorway, looking amused.

"Stop it," she snapped.

"Worried you won't be able to resist me?"

So cocky. "Worried I won't be able to resist smacking you is more like it." She stormed past him into the kitchen and yanked open her freezer.

"Krissy," he said.

"Don't." She found the sundae he'd brought for her, set it on the counter and reached into an upper cabinet for a bowl. Then she pulled out the silverware drawer and took out a sharp knife and a spoon.

"Krissy," he said again, standing closer this time.

She ignored him, ripping a banana from one of the two big bunches on her counter, peeling it, slicing it and placing the pieces into the bottom of the bowl. Then she opened the refrigerator and pulled out a container of fresh strawberries. "I'm kind of tired," she lied as she washed and sliced a few, placing them in the bowl too. "You should probably go." She scooped half of the ice cream and fudge topping into the bowl then put the rest back into the freezer.

That's when she noticed Spencer staring at her with an odd expression on his face.

"What?"

"Strawberries and bananas."

Jarrod's favorite fruits.

"Back in high school you wouldn't eat strawberries because you didn't like it when the tiny seeds got stuck in your teeth."

Still didn't like it.

"And you hated bananas, used to give Jarrod such a hard time whenever he ate one in front of you, said you couldn't even stand the smell."

Or the way they got so mushy. "Yeah. In some sick turn of events, since my morning sickness ended I crave them, can't get enough of them." She looked up at the ceiling. "I bet Jarrod's up in heaven laughing himself sick about it."

Spencer smiled. "Probably."

Krissy took a spoonful of ice cream, making sure to include some banana, some strawberry and some fudge. The flavors converged on her taste buds. Amazingly fantastic. Better than sex. Not really. Not even close. She turned to Spencer. "Why are you still here?"

"What's wrong?"

She shoved another perfectly composed spoonful of ice cream into her mouth to put off having to answer.

All too soon her mouth was empty. But when she tried to fill it again, Spencer put a hand on her forearm to stop her. "Talk to me."

Lord help her. Talking was the last thing she wanted to do with him.

Needing to say something, she looked down at her melting ice cream and shrugged. "Since Lamaze class I'm…" How to put it… "I feel…" Tense and horny and frustratingly unsatisfied.

"How do you feel?" Spencer asked quietly.

She shrugged again. "It doesn't matter." She wouldn't let it matter. "You should go."

He didn't go. "Tell me," he said, like he already knew, like he understood.

But she wouldn't be fooled. "So you can tease me?" So he could reject her again?

He shook his head, so serious.

Oh, how she wished Jarrod were here. She used to be able to tell him anything, everything. But Jarrod wasn't here. Only Spencer was, as was a lingering attraction from her youth.

An attraction she couldn't act on. He needed to go. And the best way to ensure he'd leave? Tell him the truth. In Krissy's experience, nothing made a man leave quicker than when a woman shared her innermost feelings. So she stood tall, looked him straight in the eyes, and told him the truth. "I feel tense and horny and frustratingly unsatisfied." There. Done.

She braced herself for the sting of his comeback, totally unprepared when he pulled her into his arms and said, "Me too," milliseconds before he lowered his mouth to hers.

Oh. My. God.

His lips felt warm and soft, his arms big and strong as he held her close, while being careful not to squeeze her pregnant belly.

He tightened his hold on her, moved his mouth and deepened the kiss. Pleasure took over. Need. Krissy reached up, clasped her hands around his neck and held on for the ride. This kiss had everything her kiss with Jarrod had lacked. This kiss…this soul-scorching, life-changing, earth-shattering kiss bombarded her senses like no other kiss ever had, made her feel so many things, too many things. An overwhelming intensity. An excited thrill. Affection. Lust. Anticipation. Desire. And fear.

It was too intense, too…perfect. It felt too… right, when it couldn't be right. Not with Spencer, not after all they'd been through, not after finding out what he thought of her.

She pushed him away, both of them breathing heavily.

"We shouldn't," she said. No matter how much

she may have wanted to, and she *really* wanted to, taking things one step further would make an already complicated relationship significantly more complicated.

Spencer must have thought so too because he responded with an, "I know." Then, without another word, he turned away, walked to the door, and left her apartment.

CHAPTER SIX

THE NEXT DAY, it took a monumental effort, but Spencer pushed his stupidity from the prior evening out of his mind to focus on his work. The current player on his exam table, Sergio, one of their top defenders, was suffering from an adductor strain, two weeks post injury, almost ready to return to play. Dressed in a pair of black shorts he laid on his back with his right leg bent and externally rotated, his knee propped on a balled-up towel for comfort. "How's it been feeling?" Spencer lifted the heat pack from his patient's groin.

"Better."

Most of the guys rarely complained, didn't want to spend too much time out of the lineup. Spencer would be sure to pay special attention to the patient's range of motion tolerance at the end of their session.

"Time for some therapeutic ultrasound." He

reached for the transducer. "With one finger, point to where you have the most pain."

"I don't have much pain anymore," Sergio said. "But when I do, it's here." He pointed.

Spencer spread gel on the flat transducer head and on the area Sergio had identified as most painful. Then he placed the transducer on his patient's skin, turned on the machine and set the ultrasound parameters. Keeping the transducer moving, he maintained constant contact with the skin over the localized area.

"You still taking ibuprofen?" Spencer asked.

"Every morning before coming in."

"Good."

Andres, their top scorer, recovering from a grade one inversion ankle sprain, stuck his head into the training room. "I'm finished with my exercises."

Earlier Spencer had progressed him to resistance band training. "How'd it go?"

"Still sore."

Busy with the ultrasound, Spencer told him to, "Make yourself an ice bag and ice it for fifteen minutes."

Andres did as instructed, taking the treatment table beside Sergio.

The timer dinged and the ultrasound machine shut off. Spencer wiped off the transducer head then handed the player the towel to wipe the gel from his leg. That done, he repositioned Sergio's leg and began passive stretching. "Tell me when you feel a stretch. You shouldn't feel pain."

As he applied tension, he counted off fifteen seconds then ten seconds for each rest before starting again. He pushed hard today, testing flexibility. "How's that feel?"

"Fine."

"No pain?"

"None at all."

"Good. I think tomorrow we'll head out to the field and do some work with the ball."

"Sounds good to me."

Spencer finished up then went to the sink to wash his hands. "Head on over to the weight room and get started on your exercise plan. I'll be in to check on you in a few minutes."

Around two o'clock that afternoon, Spencer had just started to clean up the athletic training room, when his cell phone buzzed in his pocket. Seeing

Krissy's name and number on the screen, he hesitated. He'd acted like a jerk last night, walking out on her without taking the time to explain... again. He debated not answering, needed more time to figure out how to apologize, how to put everything he was feeling into words, if that was even possible.

But she rarely called him. What if...? He accepted the call. "Hello?"

"Spencer Penn?"

A woman spoke. It wasn't Krissy.

"Who is this?"

"I'm calling from White Plains Hospital."

Spencer froze. "Is Krissy okay?"

Hearing a pained yell in the background, he dug into his pocket to grab his office keys and headed out the door.

"She wants to talk to you. Please hold on. A contraction took her by surprise."

Phone to his ear, Spencer hurried down the long hallway to the large lunch/meeting room, listening to Krissy's pained groans along the way. Why wasn't the nurse coaching her in Lamaze breathing?

Three of the players he'd just finished working

with stood at the far table autographing shirts and soccer balls for fans. The strength and conditioning coach sat reading the newspaper.

"Al," Spencer called to him. "I've got to take off. You'll lock up?"

"Is it time?" he asked with a smile.

A good friend, Spencer had filled him in on the situation with Krissy. "Think so."

"Good luck, man. Don't worry. I got you covered here."

"Thanks."

Brandon, the athletic training intern scheduled to work with him, sat eating a sandwich. "Everything okay?" he asked.

Phone still to his ear, trying to make out what Krissy was saying in the background, Spencer shifted the mouthpiece to answer. "Have to run." He tossed the college student his keys. "Please clean up and restock the A.T. room. Just like I've showed you." The kid had been there for six weeks. He knew what to do. "You okay on your own?"

"Yeah."

"Lock up when you're done," he said loud enough

for Al to hear. Lots of expensive rehab equipment in the A.T. room.

Al gave him a thumb's up.

"Spencer?" Krissy's voice cracked.

"I'm here."

"I know you don't want anything to do with me."

"That's not—"

She cut him off. "Déjà vu, right? Junior year of high school all over again."

"Krissy—"

"It's just, I know you're at work, but if you could spare some time. I need…" She started to cry and Spencer's heart broke. "I need…" She sniffled. "I thought I could do it on my own but…" She sniffled again in between hiccupping breaths. "Maybe you could talk to me for a few minutes, tell some jokes or something."

"Honey, it's not that I don't want anything to do with you." It was so much more complicated than that. Kissing Krissy had felt strangely dishonorable, even with Jarrod dead, same as it had so many years ago. His head and his body were not in agreement on how to proceed. He needed time to figure things out.

Time he didn't have apparently.

He turned and headed for the stairs. "How far apart are the contractions?"

"A few minutes. Oh, God. Here comes another one."

"Already?" He took the stairs two at a time. "When did you get to the hospital?"

"A few hours ago."

"A few hours? Christ, Krissy." He reached the main floor, pushed out the door, and broke into a run toward the parking lot. "Why didn't you call me?"

"Ow, ow, ow. Spencer!"

"Breathe, honey. Like this." He demonstrated, not an easy thing considering he was running as fast as he could at the same time.

"I can't," she cried out.

"You can." He reached his car, jimmed his key into the lock and opened the door. "Just like this. Do it with me." He demonstrated again.

Krissy breathed with him, her breaths strained and mixed with pained moans.

"Did you find a focal point?"

"Yes. A picture. Brought it from home."

"Good." Spencer turned on his car and hooked

up his phone so he could talk hands-free. That done, he shifted his car into drive, slammed his foot down on the gas pedal, and peeled out of his parking spot. "I can be there in fifteen minutes." If he drove through yellow lights, yielded at stop signs and ignored the posted speed limits, which he was fully prepared to do.

"Don't," she panted. "Come."

"I'm coming." He breathed with her again. "That's good. You're doing great."

"I am *not* doing great, Spencer," she yelled.

Maybe she didn't think so, but her fighting spirit told him she was doing just fine.

"It hurts." She groaned loudly.

He coached her through the pain as he pulled onto the main road. "You can do it."

"I'm so tired," she said, starting to cry again.

He hated hearing her so upset, hating knowing she had no family or friends there to offer their support. "What about pain medication? Or an epidural?"

"Natural childbirth is best for the baby," she snapped. "You know that."

Atta girl. He smiled. "So all that stuff about the unconscious birth plan?"

"Stupid coping mechanism," she said. "It's less stressful to think about taking the easy way out. But in the end, it's more important to do the right thing, which, in this case, is what's best for J.J."

Old Krissy would have taken the easy way out, regardless. "Contraction over?"

"Yes. But another one will be coming soon. My back hurts so bad."

"As soon as I get there I'll rub it."

"No, Spencer. Really. Don't come. It's too... Just talk to me. That's enough."

No it wasn't. Looking both ways, he coasted through a stop sign. "I'm coming." And that's that.

He listened on the phone, hearing only the rapid beat of the fetal heart monitor. He knew she needed to rest between contractions but couldn't stop himself from asking, "You there?"

"Of course I'm here. Where else would I be? I'm having a baby."

Spencer smiled again. "Why didn't you call me when the contractions started?"

"Because things got weird last night. Then I woke up in pain around four in the morning."

Spencer glanced at the clock on his dashboard. She'd been in labor for almost ten hours.

"How did you get to the hospital?"

"I took a taxi."

A taxi. Spencer wanted to scream. But what good would that do now? So he kept the conversation light. "Has the doctor been in?"

"I met his partner. Oh, no. Oh, God. Here comes another one."

Spencer slammed on his brakes and laid on his horn as a car came to short stop in front of him. "Idiot," he yelled.

"What?"

"Not you, honey. Bad driver." He steered around the car, sped up then stopped again, absolutely hating city traffic, even though White Plains traffic was much better than New York City traffic. "A few more minutes."

The sound of Krissy breathing through the contraction, exactly as he'd demonstrated earlier, came through his car speakers, making him so proud of her. Would this red light ever turn green? When it did he peeled out again, driving up the hill, weaving in and out of traffic. "I can see the hospital."

"Something's happening," Krissy yelled. "I have to push."

"Don't push," Spencer said at the same time a female voice, he assumed the nurse in the room with her, said the same thing. He made a sharp right then sped to the parking garage. "Breathe." He got his ticket then screeched into the structure to look for a spot. "Hang on, honey. I'm almost there."

"I'm. Not. Waiting," she said, her voice strained. Spencer heard a male voice.

"I have to—" A loud thud cut off Krissy's words.

"Krissy? Krissy! What happened?"

All he heard were muted sounds.

The next few minutes passed in a blur of stressful, heart pounding activity. Somehow Spencer managed to make it to Krissy's room before J.J. entered the world, an event he felt obligated to attend, for Krissy as much as for Jarrod.

"That's it." A male doctor, mid-fifties or early sixties, dressed in blue hospital scrubs, stood at the foot of the bed, looking down between Krissy's legs. "Keep pushing. I see the head. Push, push, push, push."

Spencer's heart started to pound for a different reason. This was really happening. Krissy was about to give birth to Jarrod's son, to Spencer's godson. The magnitude of this moment stopped him in his tracks.

"Come on, Dad," one of the nurses said. "Wash your hands then come hold her leg."

Spencer rushed to the sink without taking the time to clarify his role in all this.

He noticed Krissy didn't correct her either. Considering she was mid-contraction, she no doubt had a lot of other stuff on her mind. An intravenous ran into Krissy's right arm and an oxygen mask hung loosely around her neck. A nurse blotted sweat from her brow, something Spencer should be doing so he dried his hands, hurried to the bed, and took over for the nurse closest to him.

"Push, push, push, push," the nurse holding the other leg said.

"Come on, Krissy. You can do this," Spencer said, noticing a high school picture of him and Jarrod on the rolling table beside the bed. Had that been the item she'd chosen as her focal point?

Krissy strained and pushed.

"The head is out," the doctor said. "Stop pushing."

Spencer fought the urge to look, it just didn't feel right to be looking down there.

"I need to be done," Krissy said.

"Hey. Eyes on me," Spencer said. When her eyes met his, he said, "You're almost done. Breathe like this." He demonstrated.

She stared at his mouth and followed his lead. So focused. Absolutely amazing.

"Oh, God," she looked away. "Here comes another one."

"Give me a good push," the doctor said. "Hard as you can."

Krissy looked exhausted, but determined as she pushed harder than he'd ever seen a woman push in his life.

"You're doing it." The doctor tilted the baby and his little face came into Spencer's view, followed by his tiny body.

Unbelievable.

"It's a boy," the doctor said, placing little J.J. on paper toweling the nurse had spread on Krissy's belly.

"It's a boy," Krissy repeated, still breathing heavily, tears sliding down her cheeks. "I did it." She reached out protectively to hold J.J. steady as he cried.

"You did it." Spencer bent down to kiss her forehead. "Jarrod would have been so proud." Jarrod. The best friend he'd ever had. Jarrod, who should be here experiencing the birth of his son. This was Jarrod's dream, not Spencer's.

But Jarrod was dead.

"Want to cut the cord?" The doctor held out a pair of scissors.

With an uncomfortable hollow feeling in his gut, Spencer did what was expected of him.

An hour later, after giving Krissy privacy to clean up and breastfeed J.J. for the first time, Spencer returned to her room to find the curtain drawn around her bed.

"Oh, Krissy. He's beautiful."

He's handsome, Spencer thought, recognizing Kira's voice. Men are handsome, women are beautiful.

"I can't believe he's finally here," Krissy said, sounding tired but happy. "Mommy's going to take such good care of you," Krissy said in that voice adults used when speaking to babies.

Would she take good care of him? Or would she fall into her old party-girl ways? Time would tell.

"When you get bigger," Krissy went on. "I'll

sign you up for karate classes and soccer, just like your daddy used to take."

His daddy, who wasn't Spencer.

"But only if you want to." Her grown up voice came back. "I'm not going to force him into anything just because Jarrod liked to do it." After a brief silence, Krissy said, "What?"

"You're going to be a great mother, just like Mom was," Kira said.

"I hope so."

Spencer hoped so, too.

Through the curtain he heard J.J. start to fuss.

"Look at that face," Krissy said. "I know it makes no sense, and you're going to think I'm insane, but J.J. reminds me of Jarrod already. He makes me feel...I don't know. Having him here is...comforting. It's like a void within me has somehow been filled." She sniffled.

"Ah, honey," Kira said.

If Spencer could see through the curtain he'd bet Krissy and Kira were hugging.

"It makes complete sense," Kira said. "You and Jarrod were so close. I'm sure you miss him very much."

"Every day. I'll see something, hear something, or inhale a certain scent and I think of him."

Same thing happened to Spencer.

"I'll make sure Jarrod is never forgotten," Krissy said. "J.J. will know his daddy, he will always be his father's son, no matter what."

Spencer felt like an unnecessary outsider, an intruder, rudely eavesdropping. He should go. But there were a few things he needed to check on first. How was Krissy getting home from the hospital? Did she have everything she needed for the baby, a safe, new car seat? Diapers? Wipes? Clothes?

After something that sounded like a yawn, Krissy said, "Sorry."

"Don't be. I'm going to head to the nursery. Derrick had another newborn to visit. He should be about done. Here, let me take the baby with me. You need to rest."

Shoot, Derrick was here too? Spencer looked over his shoulder, debated the best course of action to keep from getting caught, briefly considered leaving and coming back in.

But Krissy's voice stopped him. "Derrick will do the circumcision in the morning?"

Number two on Spencer's list.

"Yes," Kira said. "Very early. Before office hours. Do you know when you and J.J. will be released?"

"I'm not sure. Probably sometime tomorrow morning."

"Call me," Kira said.

"But—"

Or she could call Spencer. He'd work it out so he could bring her home.

"Call me," Kira said again. "When you call, I'll come. I want to."

"Thank you. Here." Something jingled. "Take my keys. The car seat is in a box in the trunk."

Number one on Spencer's list, because he hadn't seen a car seat in her car or her apartment. Yeah, he'd checked. Jarrod would have wanted him to.

"Do you think Derrick will have time to install it tonight?"

Spencer had time.

"Of course," Kira said. "We'll go over when we leave the hospital and I'll drive your car here tomorrow. What else do you need?"

"Pads to put in my bra so my breasts don't leak all over."

Spencer tried to scrub that image from his brain.

"Let me write that down," Kira said.

"You and your lists," Krissy teased.

What was wrong with lists? Spencer loved lists. Speaking of which, he mentally checked off the things he'd wanted to ask Krissy that she'd already answered.

"You have a diaper pail? A baby bath?"

"No and no."

"What?" Kira asked, with the same amount of disbelief Spencer would have used had he been the one asking.

"If taking the garbage out every day doesn't work, I'll get a diaper pail," Krissy said calmly. "And for now I plan to bathe J.J. in the sink. If that doesn't work, I'll get a baby bathtub. Don't worry. I got this."

At least she'd thought it all out.

"You're good with baby clothes and supplies?" Kira asked.

"Stop," Krissy said. "A few friends had a little baby shower for me before I left Hawaii. I have what I need for now. As things come up, I'll run to the store."

Not how Spencer would have done it, but he

was a planner, liked to have everything available just in case. One of the reasons he was so good at his job.

Krissy was more of a 'deal with it when you have to' kind of person.

As much as Spencer struggled with the idea of not being prepared for every possible situation, it was Krissy's life, not his. For now, she seemed to have everything under control. He wasn't needed. He wasn't the baby's father, wasn't family, or a boyfriend, had no reason to still be there. Krissy needed to rest. So he set the flowers, the "It's a Boy" balloon, and the package of chocolates he'd picked up for her at the gift shop, down on the floor, and left the room.

CHAPTER SEVEN

TWO WEEKS LATER, Krissy stood in the doorway
to her kitchen watching Kira go through the bags
she'd lugged in and set on the table. She took out
a quart of milk and put it in the refrigerator.

"I told you the last time you brought me milk
that I don't drink milk."

"Breastfeeding women need to drink milk."

"No. They don't."

"Well, at least I know you have it available if
you want it."

She wouldn't want it. She didn't like it.

Next Kira put a package of Swiss cheese in the
refrigerator.

Krissy preferred American cheese, when she
ate cheese, which wasn't often. "I don't like you
wasting money on food I won't eat and things I
don't need."

Kira held up a bag of salad and a bottle of light
balsamic vinaigrette dressing.

"Okay. Fine. Yes," Krissy admitted, even though she didn't want to do anything to encourage her. "I like salad and that's my favorite dressing."

Looking as if she'd triumphed in battle, Kira dug into the next bag. "Look at this adorable pacifier." She held it up. "It has a baseball on the end."

"I told you I don't believe in pacifiers."

"It helps babies calm themselves down."

"So does sucking their thumb." Or in J.J.'s case, his knuckles.

Krissy struggled to generate more patience as Kira pulled out the next item, a plastic bib big enough for a toddler. "Plastic is partially responsible for destroying our environment." No, she wasn't an environmental activist to the point she'd use cloth diapers, but she limited her use of plastic when possible.

"It will keep his clothes dry when he starts teething. It was on sale," Kira said. "I couldn't resist." She held up a book on parenting. "When you're done, I'll take it."

Krissy noted the colorful strips of paper sticking out from between the pages where Kira no doubt highlighted whole sections of outdated parenting techniques. "I will raise J.J. the way I think he should be raised, not according to rules in a book that can't possibly take into consideration the unique needs of each individual child."

This interference had to stop. The time had come for Krissy to take a stand. For days she'd been trying to figure out how to broach the topic in a way that wouldn't make her seem ungrateful. They were finally on good terms and Krissy didn't want to ruin that by starting an argument. But she didn't have room for all the stuff Kira had been bringing over. She preferred to do her own grocery shopping, hated wasting the food Kira brought for her. And she would raise her son the way she darn well pleased.

"Just give it a quick browse," Kira said. "At least the chapters on teething, toilet training, and discipline. Maybe you'll learn something helpful."

Settling on the straightforward approach, Krissy started an open and honest conversation, hoping for the best. "You want to know why I decided to follow you and make a home for myself in White Plains?" At least for now.

Kira stopped what she was doing and looked up.

"To be more of a help with Mom," Krissy explained. A responsibility she'd neglected, leaving the burden on Kira for way too many years. "To be close to my only family when I gave birth to J.J. in case something horrible happened and I didn't survive, so he wouldn't be all alone. And while I appreciate every single thing you have done for me since I had J.J., I did not come here because I need you to take care of me."

"Fine." Kira started collecting the plastic bags strewn on the floor. "I won't—"

"Stop."

Kira didn't stop. "If you don't want my help," she balled up the bags and shoved them under the kitchen sink, "then I won't help."

Krissy had hurt her sister's feelings. The very last thing she'd wanted to do. "You're wonderful," Krissy told her, because she was.

Kira stopped.

"The most wonderful sister in the world." If not for Kira's fierce determination and willingness to go against the recommendations of several social workers, when she'd been only eighteen, Krissy could have been forced into foster care after their mother's severe brain injury. But Kira had held their little family together. Krissy still didn't know where she'd found the courage and stamina to do it. "But this is starting to feel like Murray all over again, and I have no intention of giving you J.J."

"Murray? My cat?"

"*My* cat," Krissy clarified. "Or at least that's how he'd started out." Krissy sat down at the table and motioned for Kira to do the same. When she did, Krissy went on, "Until you decided he should have canned food instead of dry food and he should be allowed to sleep in a bed even though I didn't want him sleeping in my bed. Until you decided I didn't buy him the right kind of toys or scoop his litter often enough or brush him often enough and you took over all of his care. Then, when we'd get into a fight, you'd bring up Murray and accuse me of being irresponsible. Well I'm not irresponsible. I just have my own way of doing things. And just because it's not the same as your way doesn't mean it's the wrong way."

Kira stared down at the table, looking deep in thought.

"When I was younger? You didn't like the way I was doing something so you took over and started doing it yourself? Fine, it was easier to let you do it than fight about it." She leaned down to catch her sister's eyes. "But I'm an adult now. It has to stop."

"I am not trying to take over. I'm only trying to help."

"By buying me milk I don't drink and cheese I don't eat."

"You're breastfeeding. You need to eat and drink healthy food. Last time I was here all you had in your refrigerator was ketchup, mayonnaise and yogurt."

"I'm only one person. I like yogurt. And when I need food I'll run to the store to get it. Or I'll order it."

Kira looked ready to argue so Krissy set her hand on Kira's forearm. "You work all day then you run to the store then you come here for a visit. Then you run home, make dinner, and spend some quiet time with Derrick before heading downstairs to Mom's apartment to check in on her. You're running yourself ragged. I know you're exhausted and more often than not, queasy. I was just recently pregnant myself, remember? I know how awful the first three months can be. And yet you're still pushing yourself. My point is, I don't want you running yourself ragged because of me. I love seeing you, but we don't have to see each other every day and you don't always have to come here. I can come to you. You don't have to make a special trip to the store for me. I'm fine. J.J.'s fine. I won't let either of us starve. I will always have a clean diaper available." And if she didn't, she'd improvise. "And if there is ever a time when we really do need something, I will call you and ask for your help." She placed her hand over her heart. "I promise."

Kira let out a weary breath. "I'm sorry. All I ever wanted to do was make your life easier than mine was."

"You have." Even if Krissy had never asked her to and she sometimes threw it back in Krissy's face. "And I love you for it. But you can stop now. I'm all grown up."

"Yes you are." Kira leaned in to hug her. "I'm so proud of the independent, competent, and hardworking person you've become."

Those words, coming from Kira, meant so much. "Thank you." Krissy hugged her back. "When you have your baby, I'm going to be there for you like you've been here for me. Every day for the first two weeks. I'm going to cook for you, shop for you, and drive you absolutely crazy with all my suggestions. Because I will finally know more about two things than you do, actual hands on taking care of a newborn and breastfeeding."

"I look forward to it."

"We'll see."

"How's it going, the breastfeeding?"

Krissy tried not to think about her cracked, sore nipples. "Let's just say it's not as natural or as easy as you'd think."

"You could…" Kira started then stopped even though Krissy could tell she really wanted to continue.

"Thank you for your restraint." Krissy smiled. "I have an appointment with a lactation consultant tomorrow."

"Good. You'll tell me how it goes?"

"Sure." Krissy glanced at the clock on the microwave. J.J. would be waking up for his next feeding any minute. "You can take back the diaper pail and baby bathtub you dropped off after I got home. I don't need them." She stood. "They're unused so you can save them for your baby. But I'm keeping the long-sleeve onesies and sleepers and the towel set."

Kira looked confused. "I didn't bring you a diaper pail or baby bath. You said if you needed them you'd buy them."

Yes, she had.

"I didn't get the other stuff, either."

"Then who?" Spencer.

Kira said his name at the same time Krissy thought it. "Spencer. At the hospital. He didn't just drop off the flowers."

And the thoughtful balloon and yummy chocolates. "He must have stuck around for a few minutes, listening." Krissy thought back on their conversation when Kira had visited her after J.J. was born, hoping she hadn't said anything about Spencer, coming to the thankful conclusion she hadn't, at least she was pretty sure she hadn't, hoped she hadn't.

"I know you had some concerns about moving into his building. Does he stop by often?" Kira asked.

Krissy shook her head. "He doesn't stop by at all." It was like he'd helped her through labor and delivery and his job was done. While part of her felt relief to not have to deal with him dogging her every move, part of her felt…deserted. Which made no sense, Spencer didn't owe her anything and they were hardly even friends. And yet...

"Not at all?" Kira clarified.

Krissy shook her head again. "But he texts me every night to see how we're doing and if we need anything, then I text him back that we're fine and don't need anything." She shrugged. "That's it." As much as she hated to admit it, she missed him. "Anyway," Krissy went on. "I'm feeling better and I'd really like to bring J.J. down to meet his grandparents."

"That's going to be such a wonderful surprise for them."

Krissy hoped so, had always thought so. But lately self-doubt had crept in, overshadowing her excitement. Should she have discussed Jarrod's request with his parents *before* she'd gone through with the artificial insemination? Should she have told them about the pregnancy *before* she'd given birth?

Too late now, she'd made her decisions and now had to live with them. "I was thinking of asking Spencer to drive me into the city. He's kept in touch with them more than I have. And I don't want to take J.J. on the train."

"I wouldn't either," Kira agreed. "If you want Derrick and me to go with you, just say the word." Kira smiled. "I'd offer to take you myself but, and I have a very hard time admitting this, I'm not a great driver and don't think I'm ready to drive into the city."

Unlike Krissy, who'd gone to college and worked outside of the city, which required she get her driver's license, Kira had lived and worked in the city up until her move to White Plains a few months ago and, thanks to public transportation, she hadn't needed a driver's license prior to that.

"Thank you." As much as she hated bothering Kira, knowing she could always count on her sister meant everything to Krissy. If J.J.'s big reveal didn't go as planned, no way she wanted to be down at Patti and Bart's apartment alone. "I'll let you know what he says." Krissy rolled her post earring between her fingers. "There's something I wanted to talk to you about," she said. Now was as good a time as any.

"Of course."

Krissy had given this a lot of thought and really wanted to know Kira's opinion. "I'd like to introduce J.J. to Mom." She shrugged. "Not that

Mom recognizes me or knows she's my mom, or that she has any understanding of what it means to be a grandmother." The traumatic brain injury had taken away so much. Krissy looked down at the table. "I just want…" *Want her to see what I've accomplished, that I'm a mother now, like her. And a good one, like she'd been. I want her to be proud of me.*

"You want…"

"Nothing," Krissy said, knowing Mom was no longer capable of noticing an accomplishment, or being proud, and she could no longer recognize the difference between a good mother and a bad mother. All she cared about were her television shows, painting and now gardening, and her beloved Oreos. Regardless, she was still Krissy's mother and Krissy wanted her mother to be a part of her son's life.

"Do you ever wonder…?" Krissy started. Then stopped, feeling foolish.

"What?" Kira asked. "Talk to me."

"Do you ever wonder if meeting our children, if finding out she's a grandma, hearing the word, will somehow trigger something deep inside…" Her eyes met Kira's. "…and bring her back to us?"

"Brain injuries are so complex. You just never know." Kira gave a slow shake of her head. "But I really don't think so."

Even though Krissy didn't think so either, hearing Kira agree wiped out the little bit of hope she'd been holding on to. "Mom would have loved being a grandmother. She'd have been fantastic at it."

Kira reached out and took Krissy's hand into hers. "It makes me sad to think our children won't know the smart, loving, exceptional woman she used to be."

Krissy blinked back tears. "That they won't get to bake cookies with her before Christmas."

"That they won't get to go out on special lunch dates with her," Kira added.

Mom had gone out of her way to make both of her daughters feel special, and loved.

"What do you think?" Krissy asked. "Is introducing J.J. to Mom a horrible idea?"

"I think…" Kira hesitated. "I think if you want to introduce J.J. to Mom, then of course you should." She released Krissy's hand and sat back. "We'll make sure to do it on one of her good days."

"How do you think she'll react?"

Now it was Kira's turn to look down at the table. "With Mom, you never know." Then she looked up. "Let's give her a few more weeks to get adjusted to her new home. Then we'll pick a time when you, me, Derrick and Tippy can all be there."

Kira didn't say it, but Krissy knew they all needed to be present in case J.J.'s presence caused Mom to act out...or become violent, which rarely happened anymore, thanks to her daily medications and the fact they'd all become so in tuned to her moods and triggers. But introducing a baby was an unknown. Who knew how Mom would react? "As much as I want to do this, I won't unless I'm sure J.J. will be safe."

"He will be," Kira said, with a confidence that put Krissy's mind at ease. "We'll all make sure of it."

The little man in question started to cry.

"Oh, good." Kira jumped up and hurried to the sink to wash her hands. "A quickie hello and cuddle with my favorite nephew then I'll leave you two in peace."

Later that evening, when Krissy received Spencer's nightly text, she responded with a return call. He answered on the first ring, "What's wrong?"

"Nothing's wrong. You asked if I needed anything and there's something I wanted to ask you."

A response would have been nice, maybe a "Sure, ask me anything." All Krissy got was silence. So she kept on talking. "I'm feeling much better now and I'd really like to take J.J. down to meet Patti and Bart. I don't want to take him on the train, and I'm not comfortable making a long trip with him in the backseat where I can't see him or take care of him if he needs me. I know this is your busy time at work, but do you think you may have a free Sunday afternoon coming up? And if you do, would you be willing to drive us in? I'd have to work it out with Patti, of course."

"Let me take a look at my schedule. If it's okay with you, I'll call Patti directly to set something up. Then I'll let you know."

"That'd be great. Thank you." Krissy hated how things felt so strained between them now. No laughing. No banter. "Don't mention J.J." Good or bad, Krissy wanted to be there in person, to see their reaction as well as to render first aid if one of them collapsed in shock.

"I won't." After a pause he added, "Thanks for asking me."

"Thanks for agreeing. And thanks for the baby bath and the diaper pail. I would have thanked you sooner if I'd known they were from you. I thought they were from Kira. We'd discussed them at the hospital."

"Uh, yeah, about that. I um…"

"No worries." She gave him an out.

He took it. "Whew. Okay, then. Well, I guess I'll be in touch with the date and time."

"Talk to you then."

Only she didn't talk to him then, because late one night about a week later, she received a text.

3 p.m. next Sunday. Pick you up at 2 p.m. Spencer.

CHAPTER EIGHT

SPENCER GLANCED AT the time on his cell phone then settled back onto his sofa. He had half an hour before he needed to head down to Krissy's apartment to get her and J.J. down to Patti and Bart's by three o'clock. He tapped his 'Find Friends' app to find her down in her apartment, where she spent most of her time, taking care of her newborn baby like a good mother should.

Maybe it'd been wrong to load the app onto her phone and accept the terms on her behalf, especially within minutes of her giving birth. But when she'd asked him to find the cell phone she'd dropped during labor, he couldn't bring himself to pass up the opportunity. When she'd moved into his building, he'd promised to respect her privacy and not to stop by without an invite. 'Find Friends' allowed him to keep tabs on her without intruding in her life, without putting them in close proximity, which would no doubt lead to more kissing, which would no doubt lead to…complications he didn't need in his life right now. The app served his needs perfectly. God willing she wouldn't notice the icon amongst the dozens already on her phone.

For all the time he spent on 'Find Friends', you'd think he was tracking more than one friend. Well, maybe tracking wasn't the best word to represent his purpose. Some might see tracking someone's movements as stalkerish behavior.

He wasn't a stalker.

He was a concerned friend, a godfather responsible for the well-being of his godson, a man trying to do the right thing while distancing himself from temptation. Yet the more he'd checked on her location over the past month, the more he'd thought about her. And the more he'd thought about her, the more he'd started to miss her. He glanced at the time again, the buzz of excitement zinging around his belly. The time had come. Today he would see her. In twenty-six minutes, to be exact. Only he didn't want to wait twenty-six more minutes. He didn't want to wait one more minute. So he stood and grabbed his keys and walked to the door.

As he left his apartment he wondered how he'd be received. After texting her every evening since she'd given birth, to see how she was doing and if she needed anything, not once had she invited him over. He should be happy, relieved even. Instead it irked him. He didn't like being shut out of her life. In the elevator he wondered if she'd be happy to see him, or angry that he showed up early, or frazzled and thankful for an extra pair of hands?

As much as he'd been thinking about her and trying to imagine what she'd look like without her pregnant belly, when she opened her door, nothing could have prepared him for the sight of her big, welcoming smile and the vision of her beautiful, voluptuous figure in a pale peach baby doll type dress, tight on top, flowy on the bottom, stopping a couple of inches above her bare knees.

All the air whooshed out of his lungs.

She looked…stunning, had lost all of her baby weight, at least as far as he could tell. But her breasts, her big, beautiful breasts had grown even larger. Spencer swallowed to keep from drooling. He couldn't look away, couldn't keep himself from thinking about dropping his head into her deep cleavage, from wondering what the soft heat of that creamy white skin surrounding his face would feel like?

"I know," she said, looking down. "They're freakishly huge."

"They're…awesome," slipped out of Spencer's mouth before he could stop himself. Thinking it made him a typical guy. Saying it out loud made him sound like a jerk.

He was on the verge of apologizing when, Krissy smiled. He took that as a 'no apology needed.'

"Come on in." She stepped aside. "We're almost ready."

The apartment wasn't as neat as it could have been, but Krissy had a diaper bag, her pocketbook, and the car seat ready and waiting by the door. J.J. looked neat and clean and way too adorable for words lying on his back on a cushiony baby comforter on the floor in the living room, just off the entryway. It didn't escape his notice that Krissy had dressed the baby in the light blue sleeper with the baseball emblem on the chest that Spencer had bought. "Wow, he's really filled out." And he was alert, his eyes opened and looking around, his little legs bending and straightening, his tiny hands clenched into fists, one shoved half into his mouth.

"He's a breast man, too," she teased, coming to stand beside Spencer. "Every two to three hours. Which means we'd better get on the road soon in case we hit traffic."

Right. But before they left, he took a few seconds to be impressed by how calm and organized she seemed.

Krissy went down on her knees and carefully scooped J.J. into her arms.

"What can I do to help?" he asked as she placed J.J. into his car seat on the floor and buckled him in.

"If you'd carry the car seat down, that'd be a big help. Usually I put him in a baby carrier thing that I wear. But since you're here I will shamelessly take advantage of your big, strong muscles."

"Happy to help," he said, meaning it. He missed helping her as much as just being around her.

On their way out the door Krissy stopped and ran back into the kitchen. "Almost forgot." She opened the refrigerator and took out a plastic bowl. "I made a fruit salad."

That she'd even thought of that, with all she had

to do, impressed him even more. "With lots of bananas and strawberries?" he teased.

"Oh, my God, don't even bring them up." The bowl in her right arm, her pocketbook and diaper bag draped over her left shoulder, she walked toward the door. "I'll start retching. Can't stand to even look at them. J.J. left my body and took those awful cravings with him." She glanced up at Spencer. "I'm hoping he doesn't develop a taste for them when he starts on solid food."

With Jarrod as his dad, chances were pretty good that he would.

Down at the parking lot, Spencer moved the base for J.J.'s car seat into his SUV. Ten minutes later they were on their way.

"I'm going to start out in the front seat," Krissy said, "So you don't feel like a chauffeur. But if J.J. starts to fuss, I may need you to pull over so I can move into the back."

"No problem."

"I hate that he has to face backward so I can't see his face."

Spencer didn't like that either. He recalled seeing a mirror that could be placed on the seat so you could see the baby's face from the front seat and in the rear view mirror. Later on he'd do an Internet search to see where he could buy one.

After he'd run out on Krissy post-kiss, then left the hospital without saying good bye, and then went a full month without seeing her, Spencer had been concerned things might be a little strained between them. But Krissy kept the conversation going, sharing stories from J.J.'s first month of life, until about halfway through their trip, when she stopped talking, mid-sentence.

Spencer looked over to see she'd fallen asleep.

So exhausted, and yet she never asked for help. Krissy was so different from his needy mother and sisters. She was so different from his last few girlfriends, too. He got the feeling Krissy wouldn't complain about his long hours on the job or days away when he traveled with the team. Krissy wouldn't demand his time and attention, wouldn't expect him to buy her expensive things she didn't need. Krissy wouldn't clam up and give him the silent treatment, either.

He smiled.

She didn't play girlie mind games. She was angry? She came right out and told you so...

loudly. That'd been one of the things he'd liked most about her.

Ten minutes from Patti and Bart's house he woke her. "Krissy," he said quietly as he gently shook her shoulder.

She jerked awake, would have sprung out of her seat if not for the seat belt. "J.J." She looked around, seeming confused.

"He's in the back. Haven't heard a peep out of him." He'd been driving with the radio off to make sure he didn't miss even the tiniest whimper. "We should be there in ten minutes."

Krissy's hand went up to twirl her post earring, a nervous gesture Jarrod used to tease her about back in high school. "You okay?"

She sat staring out the window, same as prior to Lamaze class.

He waited her out.

Still staring out the window she eventually said, "Maybe I should have checked with Patti and Bart before I went through with the artificial insemination. I mean sure, Jarrod wanted to leave a part of himself behind, wanted his parents to have a grandchild to dote on. And I grew to love the idea of having his baby, of having Patti and

Bart's grandbaby. For a long time, they were more mother and father to me than my own mother and father were. But what if they don't want a grand-child? I never once took that into consideration. What if they—?"

"Stop getting yourself all worked up. There are no two people on the planet who deserve to be and would love to be grandparents more than Patti and Bart."

"But what if—?"

"They're going to be thrilled," he told her. No doubt in his mind. "Word of advice. When Patti goes in to hug you, which she will no doubt do, I'd bet in all her excitement she's going to put some power behind that squeeze. My suggestion, take a deep breath before she grabs on to you."

Krissy's small smile warmed him.

When they reached the old neighborhood, Spen-cer circled the block to find parking. "I'm not going to find anything close. You want me to drop you—?"

"No," shot from her mouth before he could even finish. Seeming to realize her exaggerated response, she took a breath and calmed it down. "I mean, no thank you. I like to walk. Walking is good. If J.J.'s car seat is too heavy for you to carry, I'll carry it."

As if seven *maybe* eight pounds of baby and a plastic car seat would be too heavy for him to carry. Heck, he could carry Krissy and the diaper bag too without breaking a sweat. "I can handle it."

Fifteen minutes later Spencer pressed the intercom button for Patti and Bart's apartment.

"Do I look okay?" Krissy asked nervously, trying to rub some wrinkles from the front of her dress. "Do I look like a woman you'd want raising your grandchild?" she asked, without giving him a chance to respond to her first question.

"Hey," he said, lifting her chin so she had to look at him. "I know telling you not to be nervous isn't going to stop you from being nervous, but trust me, it's wasted energy. Patti and Bart love you, they've always loved you. You look beautiful. And while I find you way too sexy to want you to raise *my* grandchild, I think Patti and Bart will be perfectly fine with it."

She smacked his arm, the one holding J.J.'s car seat.

"Hey," he said. "You're going to make me drop the baby." Not likely.

Her eyes went wide.

He smiled.

She smacked him again.

Just like old times.

The intercom buzzed them in and Spencer opened the door.

"The hallway looks and smells the same," Krissy said.

Dimly lit, off-white walls with various nicks and scratches, and worn carpeting that could quite possibly be the same carpet his eleven-year-old feet had walked on so many years ago. The scents of fried food and garlic and tomato sauce lingered in the air. Coming for a visit was a journey back in time.

He tried to be a gentleman and let Krissy precede him up the stairs to the second floor, but she insisted he go first. When they reached apartment 2F, Krissy stood there, looking like she'd seen a ghost.

"You okay?" he asked her again.

"So many memories," was all she said.

So many memories indeed, delicious food, fun times and so much laughter…followed by such heart-wrenching sorrow.

After a few seconds Krissy straightened to her full height and, shoulders back, lifted her fist to knock.

Only she didn't knock. "I should probably…" She dug into her purse to take out a white business sized envelope similar to the one Jarrod had left for him. Made sense he'd leave one for his parents too. She pulled out two other papers then lifted her fist to knock again.

She hesitated.

"You want me to do it?"

She nodded.

Spencer knocked.

Bart must have been standing in wait because the door flew open. "Look at you," he said to Krissy. "Pretty as ever." He pulled her into a hug. "Haven't changed a bit."

Actually, in Spencer's estimation, she'd changed quite a bit. Adult Krissy was so much more than a pretty face, a hot body, and a fun time. She was strong and determined, yet at times, vulnerable. She was competent and responsible, yet not afraid to ask for help when she needed it. And most importantly of all, she seemed to be a great mother.

"Let them in you big oaf," Patti said from behind Bart, hitting his shoulder with a dish towel. No sooner did Bart step aside, Patti's eyes went straight to J.J., who was fast asleep in the car seat carrier dangling from Derrick's hand, and everyone went silent.

CHAPTER NINE

KRISSY SET HER hand to her chest, hoping to keep her heart from banging through her sternum, as she watched Patti set her eyes on J.J. for the first time. So many times she'd tried to visualize this moment, what Bart would say, how Patti would react. Deep down, in the tiny, still pure, believe-in-fairy-tale-endings, part of her brain that somehow remained unaffected by her years as a weary realist, Krissy had let herself believe that Patti would somehow take one look at J.J. and just know he was her grandson, that she'd feel an instant connection to Jarrod's son, an immediate grandma-grandson bond that defied rational explanation.

So Krissy wouldn't have to explain, wouldn't have to risk them not believing her. Like Spencer had.

But one look at the confusion and disbelief on

Patti's face told Krissy today would not be the day for fairy-tale endings.

Tears filled her eyes as all her dreams for the future, for happy family get-togethers, visits to grandma and grandpa's place, and over-the-top celebrations courtesy of Patti, started to flicker.

No!

In Patti and Bart's silence, Krissy couldn't help but wonder, yet again, if she'd waited too long, had missed that window of opportunity when they would have welcomed Jarrod's son? When having a grandson would have made a difference in their lives. How could she have been so stupid to automatically assume Patti and Bart would accept her child into their hearts without Jarrod being there?

Patti pointed between Krissy and Spencer. "You and Spencer...?"

"What? Me? No!" Spencer blurted. "I'm not the father."

Could he be any more insulting? He made it sound like being J.J.'s father would be the worst thing in the world. That sent tears flowing down her cheeks. She did not need Spencer tainting their view of her, making them question Jarrod's choice of a mother for his son.

She was a good mother. Maybe she didn't know it all, but every day she learned something knew, every day she strived to be better than she'd been the day before.

"Ah, honey," Patti said. "Don't cry." She held open her arms, and Krissy couldn't resist walking into them, accepting the comfort they offered.

The feel of her, so soft and cushiony, the smell of her, an elusive hint of fragrance, had Krissy feeling sixteen years old again, wanting to absorb as much of Patti's loving care as she could, to hold her through until the next time she came to visit. "I'm sorry," Krissy said, trying to keep control of all the emotion churning inside of her, looking for an outlet.

"There. There." Patti rubbed her back. "Nothing to be sorry about, having a baby is a wonderful thing. I only thought Spencer because you called looking for him. But if he's not the daddy, who is? And why didn't you bring him with you?"

Because J.J.'s daddy is dead.

With that thought the floodgates opened and months of worry and fear poured out of her, to the point she couldn't stop crying even if she wanted to. God help her it felt good, felt necessary. "I'm sorry." Her words came out between hiccupping breaths. "I waited...so long. Too long. But I...wasn't ready." She couldn't get enough air. But short of passing out from lack of oxygen, she would not stop talking, not yet, not until she said everything she needed to say. "And that I... didn't check...with you and... Bart first. But Jarrod wanted...and I agreed...and I hope..." she said, sobbing more than talking.

"Calm down, honey," Patti said. "It's okay. Everything is going to be okay."

It didn't feel okay, didn't feel like it was ever going to be okay again and Krissy's heart started to ache. What if—?

Someone walked up behind her. She heard Spencer's soft voice close to her ear, a much kinder version than when he'd balked at someone thinking he was J.J.'s dad. Heaven forbid!

"Give them the letter," he said.

Right. The letter she held in a death grip behind Patti's back. The letter that, in seeing Patti's face, she'd forgotten all about.

Krissy nodded. *Get it together.* She wiped her eyes, inhaled a shaky, yet somewhat fortifying breath and stepped away from Patti's embrace, standing tall, trying to be strong for her son. Whatever happened she'd deal with it.

Krissy handed Patti the letter. "It's from Jarrod."

From the look on Patti's face, she'd already recognized the handwriting.

"Maybe you should sit down when you read it," Spencer suggested.

Yes. Right. They should both sit down. Just in case. "In the living room?" Where she, Jarrod and Spencer had spent so many hours hanging out, watching movies or playing video games. It looked exactly the same. Pictures of Jarrod covering the far wall, his trophies and other memorabilia lining the shelving below. Bookcases filled with books lined the other wall.

As if in slow motion, Patti followed Bart into the living room and they sat down on the sofa. Wanting to give them privacy, and needing something to do, Krissy went down on her knees to unbuckle J.J. from his car seat.

Under normal circumstances, she'd have let him sleep.

These were not normal circumstances.

She needed his warmth, needed to feel him in her arms, needed to feel some connection to Jarrod. "Come on, sweetie," she whispered as he stretched and let out his little baby moans. "Time to meet your grandma and grandpa." Grabbing a shoulder cloth from the diaper bag, she lifted him. Cuddling him close to her chest, she joined Spencer by the entrance to the living room, happy to stand and sway with J.J., to burn off her nervous energy, rather than sit.

Still on the first page of the two page letter Patti looked up at Krissy. "You mean you...?"

Her expression was filled with such wonder, such hope. Krissy's eyes filled with tears again as she nodded.

"That's..." Patti brought her fingertips to her lips, her now tear-filled eyes stared at J.J.

"Jarrod's baby," Krissy said, turning J.J. to hold him in front of her, facing his grandparents, so they could get a good look at him. "Your grandson."

A jolt of fear had Krissy remembering Spencer's disbelief when she'd told him she was carrying Jarrod's baby. Not wanting to experience the same response from Patti and Bart, Krissy had come prepared. "Here." She walked to where Patti sat on the couch. "This is the documentation from the clinic where I had the artificial insemination performed, confirming the use of Jarrod's sperm. I'm not sure what he told you in the letter, but he had it frozen before his first deployment." She handed over the paper, fighting panic. *Please believe me.* "And this is the baby's birth certificate." She handed that to Patti too, not that a birth certificate served to verify paternity, but it had to mean something that she'd named the baby after Jarrod? Right?

Patti didn't scrutinize the papers like Krissy had hoped she would. Instead she handed them to Bart, still looking confused and uncertain, her eyes locked on J.J.

Krissy's hope from a moment ago turned to dread. Is this where they'd tell her they didn't believe her? Where they'd accuse her of trying to pass off another man's baby as Jarrod's, just like Spencer had? Krissy bounced J.J. while she waited for Bart to read the papers, her heart pounding in her chest once again.

"This is all my fault," Spencer said, coming to stand beside her. "Krissy's worried you're not going to believe that the baby is Jarrod's because when she told me I gave her a hard time."

A *really* hard time.

He looked down at her. "I'm sorry. Again."

"Thank you." For coming to her rescue and for the apology, but it didn't wipe his harsh words from her mind, didn't stop her from worrying.

Without a word Bart got up from the couch and left the room.

Oh, no. She glanced over to Spencer and shot him a non-verbal, *What's going on?*

Spencer shrugged but didn't look concerned.

Patti's voice interrupted the silence. "Jarrod Spencer Sadler Junior," she read from the birth certificate.

"I call him J.J."

"You gave him my name?" Spencer asked.

It'd seemed like a good idea at the time. Now? Not so much. "You're the godfather. Jarrod's other best friend. I thought…" It'd be an honor, that he'd appreciate the gesture. Apparently not.

Bart returned to the room holding a large, framed, wall-hanging picture. "Look." Patti held up the birth certificate for him to read.

The big man looked like he was barely keeping it together. "Sadler." His eyes met Krissy's. "You gave him our last name."

Of course she had. "He's Jarrod's son, Jarrod's legacy."

Bart turned the picture so Spencer and Krissy could see it. "This is Jarrod at a few weeks old."

Oh, my goodness. "They could be twins." She'd hoped there'd be a resemblance, but never did she think they'd look so much alike so early on.

"I don't need any papers to tell me that's Jarrod's child," Bart said. "I can tell from just looking at him."

Krissy thought she might melt with relief. "Thank you." Wouldn't you know it? Tears filled up her eyes again. "I'm sorry." She wiped them away, one-handed. "My emotions are all over the place lately."

"May I hold him?" Patti asked quietly, still staring at J.J., but now with such longing.

As she prepared to hand over her baby, as Patti reached out her hands to take him, Krissy saw what she'd been hoping for, waiting for. Patti looked at her grandson with so much love and pure joy it made all of Krissy's nervous concern vanish.

She handed her son to his grandma and he cuddled his little face into the base of her neck like that space had been created just for him and he'd been there a thousand times before. Patti held him close as she rocked him, eyes closed as if savoring the moment. "It feels so good to be holding a baby, again."

"To be holding your grandson, you mean," Bart said.

Tears streaming down her cheeks, Patti nodded.

"And you can hold him all you want after I get a turn." Bart held out his large hands. "Easy to forget how little they are." But he handled his grandbaby with the skill of a seasoned grandpa, and J.J. settled right in against Bart's chest, completely content.

Spencer said, "He was six pounds, two ounces when he was born."

"You were there?" Patti asked.

"Considering he bullied me into attending Lamaze classes, it seemed only fair to make him be my coach," Krissy said.

"Good for you, Spencer," Patti said. "You always were such a levelheaded boy."

Spencer smiled proudly, tauntingly, in Krissy's direction.

Krissy got the urge to stick her tongue at him in response, but she refrained.

"Oh, how I would have loved to have been there," Patti said dreamily.

"I'd gone back and forth about telling you sooner," Krissy admitted. "But I didn't want to risk you having to deal with the loss of another family member if something went wrong. So I decided to wait."

Patti stood up and gave Krissy a hug. "For as much as Spencer was the levelheaded one of your little group, you were always the thoughtful one."

She'd tried to be, still tried to be.

"You have given us the most thoughtful gift of all." Patti squeezed her tightly. "Thank you, honey. A grandchild! I can't believe it." She squeezed her even tighter. "I'm a grandma. Thank you." She kissed her cheek. "Thank you so much."

Krissy's heart swelled with love. This is the response she'd been hoping for. "You're welcome."

"Now tell me," Patti took a step back. "What do you need from us? Anything, doesn't matter how big, Bart and I will take care of it."

God how she loved this woman.

"I don't *need* you to do anything. I purposely

waited until I was mature enough and financially secure enough to raise J.J. on my own, without having to depend on anyone else. But if you *want* to do something for us, and you by no means have to, so don't feel under any pressure. I'd love it if we could get together for Sunday dinners, like we used to." Years ago.

"You don't have to go crazy cooking," Krissy told Patti. "Grilled cheese sandwiches are fine. Or take out. And it doesn't always have to be here. You could come up to my place in White Plains. It's not that far. And I have this great kitchen table we could all sit at." She slid a small smile to Spencer.

He smiled back.

"The important thing is that we're together, like family. Not that I'm family or anything," Krissy backtracked. "But J.J.—"

Patti pulled her into another hug. "I've always thought of you as family, honey, the daughter of my heart." She reached out to Spencer to include him in the hug. "And you're like a second son to me," she told him.

Spencer stepped into the hug.

Krissy started to tear up. But she had to stay

strong, had to get out what she wanted to say without falling apart again. So she stepped back and looked at Bart. "We may not *need* anything, but I'd love it if you'd teach J.J. about sports, and maybe take him to football games and baseball games." Jarrod had always looked forward to that. "And if you'd help him plan out and construct his Halloween costumes." Jarrod always had the best costumes.

"It'll be my pleasure," Bart said, cuddling his grandson close.

Krissy turned to Patti. "I'd love it if you'd make all of J.J.'s birthday cakes." Patti baked and decorated the best cakes. "And help me make his parties special. If you'd bake him your caramel fudge brownies with walnuts to celebrate soccer wins and placing in the science fair or to cheer him up after some disappointment."

Patti blotted her eyes and nodded. "Of course I will."

"But most of all, I hope your home will be a place where J.J. knows, no matter how bad life gets, he will always be welcome, he will always be safe, and most importantly, he will always be loved, like I was."

"Always," Patti said, wiping at the corners of her eyes again.

Bart sniffled and, looking down at J.J., mumbled his own, "Always."

Pure joy flowed through her veins. This was what she wanted, what she'd hoped for.

J.J. started to fuss.

"He's probably getting hungry." Krissy took him from Bart. "Is there someplace I can feed him?" She glanced between Bart and Spencer. "In private. I'm breastfeeding."

"Of course you are," Patti said. "Come." She walked toward the stairs. "You can sit in our bedroom, there's a glider rocker in there."

"Oh. I've been thinking about getting one of those."

"Well, don't you dare, Bart and I will get you one."

"You don't—"

Patti stopped and turned. "We *want* to." She placed special emphasis on 'want.' "It's the least we can do."

CHAPTER TEN

AFTER THE WOMEN retreated upstairs, Bart headed into the kitchen. He opened the oven door to peek inside, sending the delicious smell of roasting meat into the air. "She went all out for the two of you."

Spencer's empty stomach growled. "She always goes all out for company."

"Pot roast and potatoes. I can't remember the last time she made pot roast and potatoes." Bart motioned to the coffee machine on the counter. "Want a cup?"

God yes, he'd barely slept last night, thinking about today. "That'd be great."

Bart took a mug from a cabinet and handed it to Spencer. "You know your way around."

That he did.

When Spencer finished, Bart made his own cup of coffee. Then they both sat down at the table. Something about Bart's expression made Spencer uneasy. Before he could excuse himself to go…

anywhere else, Bart asked, "So what's going on between the two of you?" He followed the question with his most serious stare, the one where he locked eyes with you, trying to detect an uneasy blink, or twitch, or bead of sweat, anything that may give the slightest hint you're even considering not telling the truth.

"Nothing, sir." The truth.

Bart studied him. "Do you want there to be?"

A question that kept him up more nights than he'd ever admit. Leave it to Bart to get right to the heart of the matter. Spencer broke eye contact, dropping his head to blow on his coffee, lifting the mug to take a sip, drawing both out while considering his options, deciding there'd be no use in lying. Bart knew him too well. "Honestly?" He met the man's eyes head on. "I don't know. But for there to be something between us, she'd have to show some interest. And she hasn't." Except briefly, during their kiss.

"You've got to make her interested," Bart said, adding, "Again," in a much quieter voice.

"Again?"

"Patti and I always wondered how you could miss the way Krissy used to look at you. Weren't sure if you were too dumb to notice, or too smart to let on that you knew."

Too dumb to notice apparently. "How did she used to look at me?"

Bart looked out the kitchen window. "Like a girl in love."

Nuh-uh. No way. She'd been a flirt, a tease. She probably looked at lots of guys like a fickle girl in love.

"Oh, she loved Jarrod, too. No doubt about that. But she never looked at our son the way she looked at you." He shook his head. "The hours I had to listen to Patti fret over that. How she would have loved to have Krissy as a daughter-in-law. Alas," he took a sip of coffee. "It wasn't meant to be."

"No," Spencer said, looking into his mug. "You've got it all wrong."

"Just because you missed it, doesn't mean others didn't see it. Like Jarrod. He knew."

Spencer lifted his head.

"But he was determined, that boy of mine, thought he could create something that wasn't there."

Spencer watched him. Did Bart know Jarrod had gone into the military to impress Krissy? Yes, he did. Either Jarrod had told him or he'd figured it out, but somehow he knew.

"For a lot of years, I blamed Krissy for Jarrod's death," Spencer admitted, not able to meet the eyes of the man he'd looked up to as a surrogate father after his own father had passed away. He would be ashamed of Spencer's behavior if he knew. "When she showed up at my door, I let her know it. I was…horrible to her." He couldn't bring himself to admit the depth of just how horrible, horrible enough to send her to the hospital.

"You over it?" Bart asked with his typical straightforward approach.

Spencer nodded. "But I'm not sure she is."

"She's a tough one," Bart said. "No doubt about that. Fiercely independent. Has been for as long as I've known her. But the tough ones are worth the effort." He winked. "Make the effort." After a brief hesitation he added, "In his letter, Jarrod made it clear, if he couldn't be with Krissy, there's no one he'd want her to be with more than you."

But it wasn't up to Jarrod. "He mentioned that in my letter, too." And he just had to share that with his parents, nothing like putting Spencer under even more pressure. *Thanks, old pal.*

"Her crush on you aside, she didn't used to have great taste in men."

On that they could agree.

Without warning, Patti swooped into the kitchen. "Krissy will be down in a minute." She went straight to the drawer by the stove to take out a pad and a pen.

"Uh-oh," Bart said. "Here we go."

"You stop it." Patti sat down at the table, unfazed by her husband's teasing, and started to write. "Krissy loved the glider rocking chair that I used to rock Jarrod in."

"So give it to her," Bart said. "We don't need it."

Spencer could probably fit it in the back of his SUV. But before he had the chance to do any more than think it, Patti said, "Yes we do. For when Krissy comes to visit and when we babysit."

Bart leaned back in his chair and crossed his arms over his chest. "So it begins."

"So what begins?" Spencer couldn't help but ask.

"The lists. Everything we need to buy and everything I need to do." Bart motioned to the list Patti was feverishly making.

Spencer read: *Crib. Playpen. High chair. Bibs. Bedding. Car seat. Stroller.*

"By now she probably has all that stuff," Spencer said, even though he couldn't be sure.

Krissy entered the kitchen with a very contented looking J.J. in her arms. "All what stuff?"

"Oh, it's not for her," Bart told Spencer. "It's for here."

"What's for here?" Krissy asked, trying to catch up. Although Spencer had been present for the entire conversation and still wasn't sure what was going on.

"Go on," Bart said to Patti. "Tell them."

"All the stuff we're going to need to set up a nursery for J.J," Patti explained. "For when you come to visit." She looked over at Krissy. "For when we babysit. So you don't have to schlep."

"Give me my grandson." Bart walked over to Krissy, holding out his hands.

Krissy looked hesitant. "He hasn't burped yet."

"I'll get a burp out of him."

"Oh, he will, too," Patti said. "He's wonderful with babies."

Bart sat back down, settled J.J. against his chest with the baby's head on his shoulder, and started to pat his back very gently. Spencer watched and learned, so he'd be ready when he got a turn to hold J.J. Not today. Today was all about Patti and Bart, but someday very soon.

"So about this babysitting." Krissy pulled out the chair next to Spencer and sat down.

"We're here whenever you need us," Patti said. "Will you be going back to work?"

Without hesitation Krissy answered, "Yes. My sister has been stopping by to visit pretty much every day, but I'm not used to spending so much time at home. I need adult interaction. To be honest, I'm starting to go a little stir crazy."

Wait a minute. "I message you every evening to see if you need anything," Spencer said. "Why didn't you tell me you needed adult interaction? I would have stopped by. It's not like I have to go much out of my way or anything." Patti made a questioning face. "We're living in the same building," Spencer explained. The knowing expression on Bart's face and the hopeful expression on Patti's face had Spencer looking anywhere but at them.

Krissy said, "You always ask if I need anything, and I appreciate knowing that if and when I do, like a ride down to visit Patti and Bart for instance, I can count on you. But in the normal course of the day, I don't *need* anything. I know you're busy and you have your own life. Asking you to take time out of your day to stop by because I'm bored or lonely is selfish. Asking you to do things for me simply because I'm tired and would rather nap is inconsiderate. Regardless of what you may think of me, I'm neither of those things."

No, she wasn't, not anymore.

"I'm not your responsibility, Spencer. I don't want to be a burden."

"You're not—"

She crossed her arms over her chest. "Well then what am I? Not a friend. If I was a friend, you wouldn't have left the hospital without saying goodbye."

"You needed your rest." It sounded lame, even to his own ears.

"If I was a friend," she went on. "You would have stopped by my apartment to visit me, and I haven't seen you in a month…not until I *needed* you for something."

Oh, no. "I was trying not to bother you. I was respecting your privacy and waiting for you to invite me over, like I'd promised I would do when you moved into my building."

She studied him. "You mean you *wanted* to…?"

He nodded.

She smiled. "Then instead of texting me to see what I need, you should have sent me a text that said: No plans tonight, you want to do pizza and a movie at your place? And I would most likely have responded with a: Heck yeah! What time?"

Good to know.

"What will you do for child care?" Patti asked.

"Well that's the million-dollar question, isn't it?" Krissy said. "I'm lucky that Jarrod's generosity has given me a financial cushion so I don't have to go back to work right away. But I enjoy working as a nurse and I'm eager to get back to it. Plus I want to save as much of that money as I can for J.J.'s future."

"I wish we lived closer," Patti said. "I would give up my job to babysit my grandson in a heartbeat."

The two women chattered like they were the only two in the room, like they used to years ago, while Spencer and Jarrod played video games and Bart, when he was home, sat in his recliner chair, reading. Back then, Spencer had listened with half an ear, if he'd listened at all. Today he paid close attention.

"Would I be a terrible person if I admitted to hoping you'd feel that way?" Krissy asked. "But I know. The distance is a problem. I've thought about moving back to the city, maybe getting a place close by."

What? No. Spencer didn't like the thought of that at all. He liked seeing her car in the parking lot, being able to check the tires and registration/inspection stickers to make sure she was driving little J.J. around in a safe vehicle. He liked being close by, liked knowing that her levelheaded sister played a big role in her life.

"But that'd be expensive," Krissy noted.

Right. Very expensive. Don't do it.

"My sister is pregnant," she went on. "My mom lives with her and I really feel the need to be close to both of them, if I can manage it."

Oh, she'd be able to manage it. Spencer would see to it. Somehow.

Patti shared a look with Bart that Spencer couldn't quite read. But Bart's nod showed he understood and agreed.

"You've got time, honey." Patti reached out to pat Krissy's hand. "Don't rush into anything. Let us know before you make any major decisions. I bet between us we can figure something out."

J.J. let out a loud, rather impressive, burp.

"Atta boy," Bart said every bit the proud grandpa.

"Well done," Patti said. And she actually clapped.

"Hey." Spencer would have none of that. "Since when is it acceptable to burp at your table?" More than a few times he and/or Jarrod had been banished to the living room as punishment for burping, even when they hadn't done it on purpose. He turned to Krissy. "My how things have changed."

Making her smile was fast becoming his new favorite thing.

Patti waved a threatening finger at him. "Now don't you go thinking *you* can do it!"

The grandbaby fed, changed, and burped, they were finally ready to adjourn to the dining room for dinner. A brief argument ended with Krissy convincing Patti she needed two hands to eat and J.J. would be fine laying on a cushiony blanket on the floor between them, set back a little from the table so nothing would spill on him.

Spencer had attended Sunday dinner at Patti

and Bart's numerous times over the years since Jarrod had died, and no dinner had been more enjoyable than this one. Adding Krissy and J.J. to the mix lifted the mood and increased the fun factor considerably.

But all too soon it was time to say goodbye.

Patti and Bart walked them to the car, probably to spend every minute they could with J.J. which was fine with Spencer, since Bart carried the car seat and all he had to carry was the leftovers.

Back in his SUV, with Krissy settled into the front passenger seat, Spencer said, "That went pretty well, don't you think?"

Her head back against the seat, she nodded, looking tired.

"Did Patti really ask if she could Skype with J.J.?"

Krissy smiled and nodded again. "Yup."

"Don't worry." He patted her thigh. "It's all so unexpected and new. They'll calm down." Eventually.

"I hope not. I want them involved. I want J.J. to have what Jarrod had." She took his hand—which somehow still rested on the bare skin just above her knee—and held it. "Thank you so much for coming with me." She looked up at him. "I really needed you there."

"Happy to be of service." What an asinine thing to say. He squeezed her hand. "Thank you for asking me to go with you. I really wanted to be there."

Krissy covered her mouth with her free hand as she yawned. "Sorry. J.J.'s still getting up two, sometimes three times a night. Derrick suggested I consider giving him a bottle of formula at bedtime to see if he'll feel fuller and sleep longer. But I'm not ready for that." She yawned again. "Last night I couldn't get myself back to sleep between feedings. Worried about today."

Understandable. "Go to sleep." He released her hand. "If J.J. needs you, I'll wake you up."

She looked up at him with sleepy eyes. "Thank you."

"Oh, before I forget."

She opened her eyes.

"Thank you for giving J.J. my name, too." After hearing that, he felt even more of a bond between him and his godson. "It really means a lot." More than she could ever know.

She smiled. "I'm glad. You're going to be a great godfather, Spencer."

He planned to be.

Her eyes drifted closed again, and she slept for the rest of the trip.

After carrying J.J. up to Krissy's apartment and saying good night to both of them, Spencer stood in the hallway outside of her door and took out his phone to text her.

No plans Tuesday night. You want to do pizza and a movie at your place?

He hit send.

She responded before he made it to the elevator.

Heck, yeah. What time?

He smiled.

7:30. I'll bring the pizza.

It's a date! See you then.

CHAPTER ELEVEN

IT'S A DATE. Why the heck did she have to call tonight a date? Krissy hurried around her apartment, plucking clothing and assorted baby paraphernalia from the couch, floor, and basically every flat surface around her apartment. Did Spencer think it was a date? She walked into her bedroom and dumped everything on the bed.

Did he want it to be a date?

Did she?

The memory of that kiss they'd shared in her kitchen sent warm tingles of joy and anticipation pulsing through her body. Part of her, a long neglected part, sure wanted tonight to be a date.

"Stop it," she whispered so as not to wake J.J. who lay napping in his crib in the bedroom they shared. "It's not a date."

But then she turned and caught a glimpse of herself in the mirror, hair scrunched perfectly, cute little pink sundress, and makeup. Yes, she'd actually made time to apply makeup and shave and paint her toenails. She looked down to admire her skill, such a pretty shade of pink.

"I should change," she told her reflection in the mirror above the dresser. "Into sweats." As quietly as she could, she eased out a drawer. "Something that'll make it clear I'm not trying to impress him." Only she was trying to impress him.

A knock on her front door brought the decision of what to change into to a halt. She glanced at her alarm clock. "What is it with that man always coming early?" She left the room, leaving the door ajar, and then went to greet Spencer.

Deciding it didn't matter how she looked or what she wore as long as she set him straight right from the start, Krissy opened the door, and before saying 'Come in' or 'That pizza smells great' or even 'Hello,' she said, "This is not a date. I know in my text message I said it's a date, but it's not a date."

Spencer stared at her.

His lack of response sent her into full babble. "Unless you want it to be a date, in which case I guess it could be a date." She looked up at him. "Did you want it to be a date?"

"I want it to be whatever you want it to be," he

said calmly, almost cautiously, as if worried saying the wrong thing might launch her into crazy town.

"All right then." She took a deep breath then let it out. "Not a date." She stepped back to let him in. "Just dinner and a movie with a friend. Purely platonic."

"Works for me." He walked into the kitchen and set the pizza box on the counter. "Where's the little man?"

She liked that, 'the little man.' "He's totally off schedule today. I have no idea why or how long we'll have until he wakes up. We can eat in here and I doubt I'll make it through the whole movie without having to feed him. Or we can eat on the coffee table and start the movie now."

"Let's eat in the kitchen. I don't mind pausing the movie later on if we need to."

She appreciated that.

While he washed his hands, she set the table. They both reached for the pizza box at the same time, in the exact same spot where he'd kissed her. Krissy froze, which was odd, considering everything inside of her warmed most pleasantly.

Spencer went still.

He looked down.

She looked up.

Their eyes met.

"You worried I'm going to kiss you again?" he asked.

"More like worried you're *not* going to kiss me again."

He smiled.

Uhhh… "Did I say that out loud?"

His smile widened. "Yes, you did."

She blamed, "Pregnancy brain. I'm breastfeeding so things aren't back to normal yet."

He leaned in, slowly, no longer smiling, his mouth getting closer.

She should stop him, stop this craziness. This kiss, that she wanted with every fiber of her being, could ruin the fragile friendship between them. If he walked out on her again… His lips millimeters from hers she said, "A word of warning, Spencer."

He stopped, but held his position.

"If you kiss me and leave again, I'll consider this your third and final strike. I will never again give you the opportunity—"

He closed the small distance between them, setting his lips to hers, gently, sweetly, but oh, so enticingly.

It wasn't enough.

Krissy's body screaming for more, she went up on her tiptoes, wrapped her arms around his neck, and pulled him close.

Much better.

Spencer's hands caressed down her back to cup her butt. "Too much?" he asked against her lips.

"No." She answered. *More.*

He yanked her hips in tight to his.

Just right.

Or so she'd thought, until he dipped his tongue into her mouth again and again, tasting her, and, she'd like to think maybe savoring her a little, too.

Perfect.

But all too soon the kissing stopped and Spencer moved his mouth along her jaw, to her ear. "Pizza's getting cold," he whispered.

His scruff tickled her skin. That combined with the aftermath of their kiss and his heated breath on the inner rim of her ear made her eyes go blurry. She tried to focus. "There's pizza?" Pizza was not what her body wanted at the moment.

Spencer smiled against her cheek. "Come on." He left her to carry the box over to the table. "Let's eat."

But Krissy wasn't able to change gears so quickly.

"That was some kiss." She traced her still tingling lips with her index finger.

"There's more where that came from," Spencer said as he served himself a slice of pizza then put one on her plate as well. "But I figure it's best we stop now, since tonight we're keeping things platonic."

He deserved a nice, hard pinch, and Krissy was more than willing to give him one. Instead she goaded him right back. "Interesting plan." She sat down. "Although most men I know take what they can get when they can get it."

"I'm not most men."

No. He certainly was not. Most men would not accompany a woman they hadn't seen in years, and didn't much like, to Lamaze class. Most men would not leave work and speed across town to attend the birth of a baby that wasn't theirs. Most men would not give up their very limited free time to drive a friend into the city then stick around for the emotional tear-fest when she introduced her baby to his grandparents for the first time. "No." She met his eyes. "You're not most men."

"Thank you for noticing." He took a bite of pizza.

For some reason she hadn't noticed…until that moment. Sure, she'd found him physically attractive from the start. But noticing his other very attractive qualities, his confidence, dependability, and attentiveness had taken a bit longer. Needing to process that bit of newly recognized information, Krissy took a bite of her own pizza so she wouldn't have to talk.

Spencer filled the quiet. "So how is it a pretty, fun, sassy woman such as yourself doesn't have a grown-up man in her life?"

Unfortunately that was easy enough to answer. "I've had a few boyfriends over the years, some relationships longer and more serious than others." She took a sip of water. "Some didn't work out. Others…who I thought maybe…dumped me when I told them about Jarrod and my plan to have his baby."

"A bunch of idiots." He took a bite of pizza.

How sweet of him to say so. "Jarrod would have thought so, too. Now your turn." She looked him in the eyes. "You're good looking and you've got the whole good-guy vibe buzzing around you. How come no woman has claimed you as hers?"

He raised both eyebrows and tilted his head at her. "Good-guy vibe?"

"I know." Krissy took a small bite of her own pizza. "Caught me by surprise too." And very recently, as a matter of fact.

"I dated my last girlfriend for two years."

That shouldn't make Krissy jealous, yet it did.

"A year and a half too long," he admitted.

That made her feel better.

"She started out sweet. But the longer we were together the more demanding she got, always nagging me to spend more time with her. The needier she got, always asking me to do things for her. Between her, my mom and my sisters, and my new job with NYC United, something had to give. So I broke up with her."

"Two things I will never be, demanding and needy." Krissy felt his stare and looked up. "What?"

"Two things you will never be, demanding and needy?"

"I said that out loud?"

He nodded, looking way too amused. "Apparently so, because I heard it. And it's got me wondering why you'd be comparing yourself to my last girlfriend?"

Krissy shrugged. No particular reason.

Spencer studied her, waiting for a response.

Krissy didn't have a good response available at the moment, so she pretended to listen carefully, going as far as to squint her eyes and turn her ear toward the hallway. "I think I hear J.J." She stood and left the kitchen. Not because she'd heard J.J., who lay sleeping in his crib like a little angel, but because she needed a few minutes to regroup.

Why on earth had she compared herself to Spencer's last girlfriend? That answer came easily enough: To tell him she'd never be demanding and needy. Why did she want him to know she'd never be demanding and needy? No way. She refused to accept the first answer that came to her. Maybe standing alone thinking wasn't the best course of action at the moment.

Returning to the kitchen, Spencer's expression told her he knew exactly why she'd left. But he played along anyway. "Everything okay with J.J.?"

"Yup." She sat back down, no sense saying any more. He'd know she was lying. "So how's work?"

Soccer was a much safer topic than past relationships. "The team's playing well. Alfonso has made a huge improvement to your wins and losses record."

Luckily Spencer loved talking about soccer, and Krissy knew just enough to ask the right questions to keep the conversation going. Before long they'd wrapped up the leftover pizza, cleaned the kitchen, and were on the couch ready to start the movie.

Turning off the lights in the living room and closing the blinds in an attempt to recreate an actual movie-going experience, sans the massive screen and surround sound, had seemed like a good idea…until Krissy seated herself next to Spencer, the two of them alone, in a room lit only by her television screen.

She'd let him pick the movie, didn't really matter what they watched on account of she felt hot and horny and all she could think about was how easy it'd be to straddle his lap to rock and rub…

"You don't like the movie," he said.

"The movie is fine." It was his proximity that was giving her trouble. Like in Lamaze class, proximity had given him an impressive erection.

Proximity had him claiming he could get her off in minutes, in a room full of people without anyone knowing. Right now, the 'get her off in minutes' part had her concentrating on that possibility rather than the movie.

Spencer laughed.

Krissy looked at the television.

"You didn't laugh," Spencer said. "Everyone laughs at that part."

She hadn't laughed because she hadn't seen or heard what had happened on screen because she'd been too busy imagining what it'd feel like to have Spencer's hand in her panties, to have his erection deep inside of her, pumping… She inhaled a shaky breath.

This had to stop.

Spencer picked up the remote control from the coffee table and paused the movie. Then he turned to look at her. "What's wrong?"

Shrugging seemed easier than having to answer, so that's what she did.

"Not good enough," Spencer said.

Pain in the butt. "Just thinking about something, that's all."

Please leave it at that. Please leave it at that.

He didn't leave it at that. "Thinking about what?"

Of course he'd ask. And you know what? Of course she'd answer. With the truth. Krissy didn't let guys get her all…befuddled. What the—? Krissy also never used the word befuddled. "Fine. You want to know what's on my mind?"

He nodded. "Yes. That's why I asked."

Well get ready for an honest response. She looked him straight in the eyes. "At Lamaze class, you said you could get me off in minutes, in a room full of people without anyone knowing. Were you serious?"

"That's what you're sitting here thinking about? Me getting you off?"

Not proud of it, at all, but yup.

"Good," he said. "You and your 'Those rumors back in high school were true. I give an amazing blow job.' How is a man supposed to sit next to you, in the dark, without thinking about that? But you said platonic." He threw that back at her.

Staring straight ahead she asked, "What if I changed my mind?" Out of necessity. Out of desperation.

Spencer shifted on the couch, ever so slightly. "Then I'd say, for the record, I told you I could get you off in minutes, in a room full of people if you could keep it quiet, which I seriously doubt."

Was that a challenge? "Oh, I can keep quiet if I want to keep quiet." Except where was the fun in that?

"Really?" He moved fast, reaching out, lifting her onto his lap, facing toward the television. "Let's see." He draped her legs over his then started to spread them, slowly, carefully. "This okay?"

"Yes."

He kept going until her legs were spread as wide as they could go. "Lean back."

Primed and eager to see where this would lead, she did, resting her back on his chest, her head on his shoulder.

A moment of hesitation, of worry that letting Spencer proceed was a mistake of epic proportions, fled the instant his warm fingers took a gentle glide from her inner knees up the sensitive insides of her thighs to the elastic leg openings of her panties. Yay for wearing a dress!

"Is it okay if I touch you?"

"Yes." Please do, right away, and hurry it up if you don't mind.

He dipped beneath the elastic, following it up to her hips then down as low as he could reach.

It was all Krissy could do not to cry out at the overwhelming sensation of being touched by a man's hands, so intimately after so long. But she wanted more, needed more, now, so she tried to shift on his lap, to get him to—

"Nu, uh, uh," he said quietly, his mouth next to her ear. "I'm in charge."

Oh, no, sirree. Krissy tried to sit up. She had no intention of letting him—

"You want me to stop?" he asked.

God, no. Her body plopped back down of its own accord. "I'm not one to just lie in one spot without moving."

"Shh…" he whispered. "Pretend we're in a room full of people. No moving and no talking."

"Then hurry up," she whispered back, losing patience with this game, ready to excuse herself to the bathroom to take care of things on her own.

"Tsk, tsk, tsk," he moved his hands, sliding both down beneath the top of her panties this time. "And you told me you weren't demanding."

She rocked her hips, urging them upward, inviting him in, so close. "I'm usually not. But sometimes…"

He pushed forward, between the seam of her lips to her opening and Krissy lost all control, needed this, so bad. "Yes. Like that." She moved up he moved down. She moved down he moved up, over and over again. "Soooo good." He spread her wetness, moved his hand faster, in circles.

Absolutely shameless, Krissy rocked her hips, rolled her hips, arched her back, getting closer. "I need more."

"Tell me what you need."

"Harder. Move faster, side to side." He did. "Inside. I need you inside."

He stopped.

"Noooo!"

"Is it okay?"

"Yes. It's okay. Please."

"Have you been to the doctor? Did *he* say it's okay?"

"God, I hate you."

She tried to sit up.

He threw his arms around her and held her tight. "Don't go. Let me take care of you." He slid one hand back between her legs, swirling the tips of his fingers around her opening, turning Krissy into a limp rag of compliance.

"That's my girl."

She wasn't a girl, only she couldn't muster the muscle control necessary for speech to tell him so. Later. She'd tell him later. Much later. Right now... "God that feels good. Don't stop."

He didn't stop.

Lungs heaving, orgasm building, Krissy lost herself in the pleasure, moving as her body needed to move, moaning when she needed to moan, until it happened, that burst of wonderfulness that had her crying out, "Yes! Oh, God, yesssssss!"

"Shh," he said, but he kept moving until every last bit of pleasure had been drained from her sated body, until Krissy drifted off into a blissful place she never wanted to leave.

Spencer's kisses to her cheek and neck brought her back, which was when she noticed the swell of his erection beneath her butt.

His turn.

She got up carefully, making sure her legs would hold her, before she stood and stripped off her saturated panties.

"We can't," Spencer said.

As much as she wanted to, she hadn't been to the doctor yet, hadn't been given the all clear to resume sexual activity. So she dropped to her knees at his feet, pushing his legs apart to make room for herself.

"What are you doing?" he asked, watching her every move.

She let her actions answer, unsnapping the button of his jeans, working down the zipper, and exposing the tip of his cotton covered sex. She dropped her mouth down to kiss it. "Getting acquainted."

CHAPTER TWELVE

GETTING ACQUAINTED? KRISSY blew out a hot breath, barely filtered through his cotton briefs, and Spencer thought both of his heads might explode. "You don't have to." But every single cell in his body wanted her to, needed her to.

"Lift up."

At this point he'd do anything, absolutely anything, to feel her hot, wet mouth on the bare skin of his erection. He followed her instruction, lifting up and helping her slide his jeans and underwear over his hips, exposing that part of him, allowing it to stand tall and proud, eager and ready.

"Well look at you." Krissy caressed him with her soft hand, from tip to base, applying just the right amount of pressure. "Spencer Penn is all grown up."

In the process of formulating a comeback, his mind went immediately blank when she sucked him deep, taking all of him, and holding him there, squeezing him there, down into her throat.

Spencer fought to remain still, when every part of him wanted to thrust into her, hard and fast.

When she started to move, Spencer thought he might weep with joy. And he was *not* the weep with joy type. Krissy moved on him like a woman on a mission, a mission he fully condoned and was thrilled to be a part of, taking him deep again and again.

"That feels…" No word seemed adequate. He settled on, "Fantastic." He didn't want to waste valuable energy thinking.

Her hands worked in tandem with her mouth, her talented tongue swirling around his tip before she dove back down his length.

He fisted his hands on the couch, didn't want to touch her, didn't want to do anything that might interfere with the perfection of her mouth on him and the rhythm she'd set, a perfect rhythm that had his balls starting to tingle a most enjoyable warning of spectacular things to come. So good, too good. "I'm not going to last." He didn't want to last, not this time.

God love her, she seemed okay with that.

Spencer lost the battle to control his hands and they gripped her head as his hips lifted in jerky little thrusts, up and in, a little deeper each time, he couldn't help it. "Oh, God." Feet planted on the floor, he moved faster, couldn't stop. "Oh, God. Here it comes." He tried to lift her off of him but she fought back, sucking him deep again and again until he gave her every bit he had to offer, the intensity of his orgasm draining him of the ability to do anything but exist in a place of over-whelming contentment.

Until J.J. started to cry.

"Perfect timing," Krissy said, standing up.

Spencer forced his eyes open to see her wiping her mouth.

"No time for first time post orgasm awkward-ness with a baby in the next room." She forced a playful smile, all lips.

She looked nervous and uncomfortable and Spencer hated that.

"Come here." He grabbed her hand and pulled her down for a kiss. "I like tasting myself when I kiss you."

She pushed away and stood. "You probably want

to get going." She bent to pick her underwear up from the floor.

"Don't do this," Spencer said, not when their shared intimacy had made it clear he could have a relationship with her based on more than Jarrod wanting them together and Spencer's feeling responsible for J.J. He tugged his briefs and pants back up. He'd grown to like her again, but more importantly, he'd grown to respect her. Friendship, respect, and mutual attraction made a strong foundation for a lasting relationship. This could work. "I'm not feeling awkward." He was feeling supremely satisfied, hopeful for the future, and maybe a little sleepy, but most definitely not awkward. "You shouldn't feel awkward either."

"I'm not sure how to do this," she said.

"I beg to differ." He stood. "In my opinion you were great at it." He kissed the top of her head then moved to see her face, liking the shy smile he saw there.

"Yeah, I guess you were pretty good at it, too. But I was talking about us." She motioned between them. "You and me and whatever's happening between us. What if—?"

J.J. started to cry louder.

"Go take care of him," Spencer said. "We can talk more when you're done."

"I have to change him and feed him. It takes a while."

"If you feed him out here, on the couch, I promise not to look." She had no idea the magnitude of restraint that would require. He'd been dreaming about her breasts, seeing them bare before him, touching them and sucking their nipples, since he'd hit puberty.

He started to get hard all over again just thinking about it.

While Krissy took care of J.J., Spencer took some time to clean up and get himself back under control. Apparently that took the same amount of time as a diaper change because he returned to the living room at the same time Krissy exited her bedroom carrying a wide awake J.J.

"Hey there, big guy." Spencer rubbed his back. "Hungry?"

J.J. started to squirm.

Krissy walked toward the couch. "He's not much for social interaction when his stomach's empty."

Spencer turned on the movie, but lowered the

sound, not so he could listen to J.J. feeding. That was an added bonus.

He sat there, staring at the television, not watching the action on the screen, lost in thought, feeling... He couldn't quite summarize how he was feeling. Content. Happy. Protective. *Is this how men feel while sitting beside their wives, listening to their son's voraciously taking nourishment from their wives' bodies?* It felt good.

Except Krissy wasn't his wife, and J.J. wasn't his son, and this had been Jarrod's dream, not his. But Jarrod wasn't here to live out his dream. Could Spencer take it on as his own?

"You're staring."

Unintentionally. Somehow it'd just happened. Rather than delve into the thoughts racing through his mind, thoughts that had somehow, unbeknownst to him, turned his head, he decided to make light of getting caught. But not until he took a moment to really see the beautiful sight before him. The top of Krissy's dress unbuttoned, her left breast exposed with J.J. latched on to the nipple. "Can you believe I'm jealous of a five-week-old baby? What does that say about me?"

Krissy smiled. "That you're a breast man?"

Oh, yeah. For sure. He nodded, preferring to think about that rather than all the other stuff.

"Well, sorry to say," she looked down at her son and caressed the top of his head lovingly. "Right now my boobs are for nutritional enrichment only."

"I'm a patient man," he told her, even though right now he didn't feel like a patient man. "I can wait." And dream and anticipate and plan all the things he would do when he could finally see them, feel them and taste them.

Since thinking carnal thoughts of a breastfeeding mother felt wrong, on so many levels, Spencer turned his attention back to the television set, and raised the volume enough to cancel out the sounds coming from beside him. Eyes focused straight ahead, Spencer tried to ignore Krissy removing J.J. from her breast and shifting him to feed on the other side. He only knew what was happening thanks to his excellent peripheral vision.

The baby's soft head brushed up against his a forearm.

"Sorry," Krissy said. "I'm not used to doing this while someone else is on the couch."

He wanted to say, "Well get used to it because

I plan to be hanging around a lot more often." Instead he said, "No worries."

A few minutes later, movement caught his attention again. "Is it okay to look?"

"I'm…almost…yes."

He turned to see her buttoning her dress. "Do you want me to burp him?"

She'd gone from them fooling around on the couch to change J.J. then back to the couch to feed him without ever using the bathroom, putting the needs of her son ahead of her own. "You don't mind?"

"Of course not." He'd do whatever he could to help her.

With a relieved smile she said, "That'd be great." She handed him a white cloth. "Put this on your shoulder."

Spencer thought back to how Bart had done it, and when Krissy handed him J.J., he held the baby the exact same way.

"Just rub and pat."

Spencer rubbed and patted.

"He won't break."

"Good to know."

With another beautiful smile, she turned and

after going into her bedroom for a moment, she walked across the hall into the bathroom.

"Just you and me," he told J.J., feeling a little nervous about holding his godson in his arms for the very first time, not that he'd ever tell Krissy that. He rubbed and patted and nothing happened.

J.J. started to fuss.

Spencer stood, swaying in place like he'd seen Krissy do down at Patti and Bart's. He continued rubbing and patting and was rewarded with a very loud burp.

"Good job." J.J. calmed right down after that, and Spencer felt quite a sense of accomplishment. It felt good to hold a baby and take care of him, and not just any baby, Krissy and Jarrod's baby. His godson. "If there was any way your daddy could be here with you right now, he would be. But don't you worry that he's not here, because I am and I'll always be here for you."

A noise brought his attention to the hallway, where Krissy stood, watching him from the shadows.

"Sorry," he said, because an apology felt necessary for some reason. "I didn't mean—" that he planned to replace Jarrod or...

Before he could finish that thought Krissy was hugging him. "Thank you."

Thank you? "For what?"

"For showing me the kind of godfather you plan to be, for talking to J.J. about his dad. For coming to hang out with me tonight, and not leaving when I had to nurse, and…for everything else."

Holding J.J. in his left arm and Krissy in his right, Spencer felt a part of something special, a part of this little family. And he liked it.

Krissy said, "Let's see if you can put J.J. down in his crib without him waking up."

Spencer felt like he could do anything.

Except, it seemed putting a baby down into a crib, without waking him, required special skills. Luckily, Krissy possessed those skills, and quickly took over, whispering, "Wait for me in the living room," as she quieted her crying baby.

Okay. Spencer walked into the hallway. He wasn't a perfect surrogate parent, not yet, anyway. It would take time. He had no problem putting in the time it would take to master the task, in fact, he looked forward to it.

Krissy emerged from the bedroom a few minutes later, looking tired. "If you're okay with me possibly falling asleep on you, you're welcome to stay and finish the movie."

He didn't care about the movie. But cuddling on the couch with a sleepy Krissy sounded most appealing. "Sure." Since he was already sitting on the couch he lifted his arm, inviting her to slide on in next to him.

She did, setting her head on his shoulder, fitting in beside him like the curves of his body had been created just for her. He clicked on the movie, but didn't watch. Instead he closed his eyes, savoring this moment of absolute perfection.

Krissy dozed off within seconds of sitting down.

Spencer sat there, holding her, eventually shifting their positions so she laid half on top of him. He would have stayed there, just like that, all night, but he had to work in the morning. Planning to carry her to bed, Spencer slid off the couch, trying not to wake her.

"What?" Krissy sat up.

"Sorry. I tried not to wake you."

She rubbed her eyes. "What time is it?"

"A little after midnight, I've got to get going."

Krissy stood. "I'll walk you to the door."

"We have a rare Wednesday night game tomorrow so I won't be home until late. Are you free Thursday? I could pick up dinner and—"

Krissy put her hand on his chest. "I don't expect you to stop by every night to see me. Don't feel like you have to explain your schedule to me. We fooled around, that's it, nothing more."

It meant more to him. But he wasn't ready to tell her that just yet. "While I appreciate you not expecting me to stop by every night, I'd like to stop by when I can. Would that be okay? If I check with you first?" He didn't want to crowd her.

She nodded. "That'd be great."

Good. "So." He tried to sound casual. "Any doctor's appointments coming up?" He slipped on his shoes to avoid looking at her.

J.J. would be turning six weeks old next week which meant Krissy should be due for her six week checkup at the OB-GYN. According to his research, that's the appointment where a woman who had a normal vaginal delivery was usually cleared to resume sexual intercourse.

When he looked up, Krissy smiled. "Why Spencer Penn, are you asking because you want to have sex with me?"

Heck yeah! "After tonight, there should be no

doubt in your mind that I'm attracted to you. God's honest truth, I want to make love to you more than I've ever wanted to make love to any other woman in my entire life. That doesn't mean I'm going to pressure you or expect anything based on tonight's…fun. It's just, if we should wind up alone and in the mood, *again*, and we both want to take things further than we did tonight, I want to know that you've been medically cleared to do so. That's all."

"Since you're planning to stop by a lot more often, I'm guessing chances are high we'll wind up alone and in the mood again soon."

"Exactly." Whoa. "Wait a minute. That's not why—"

Krissy smiled. "I know, Spencer." Then she wrapped her arms around his neck, went up on her tiptoes and whispered, "I have an appointment next Thursday." She tongued his ear. "And I'd love for you to be the first guy I'm with post baby. I trust that you'll, you know, take it easy until we're sure everything on the inside is all healed up and back to working like it should."

First guy? First *and* last he thought, feeling

rather territorial even though he had no right to be. He hugged her close. "You know I will."

"You have any plans for Thursday night?"

Didn't matter, if he did, he'd cancel them. "Now I do."

"Bring condoms."

Lots and lots of condoms. Check!

She released him. "And Spencer?"

"Yeah."

Her eyes met his. "If we take this next step, please promise me that, no matter what happens, you won't start to hate me again."

"I promise." On Jarrod's grave, he promised.

After that, Spencer visited Krissy almost every night. They ate dinner together, talked about their days, and laughed, a lot. Then they cuddled on the couch, exploring each other's bodies, never to the point of orgasm. They'd agreed to save that for when he could be buried deep inside her.

At Sunday dinner with Patti and Bart, they acted like there was nothing starting up between them. Krissy had felt it was too new, she didn't want the pressure of Patti and Bart hoping for something permanent between them. It was too late for him to escape it. At least he could save her for the time being. So he'd played along while under Patti and Bart's watchful eyes. But he'd held her hand during the car ride down and then back home again. And when they'd slipped out to take a walk to the local park, just the two of them, he'd kissed her under the tree where she, he, and Jarrod used to hang out as pre-teens, acting too old for the swings and slide.

On Thursday, Spencer made sure to clear his schedule around noon, expecting to hear from Krissy. When his cell phone vibrated in his pocket, he jammed his hand in there to retrieve it.

Just saw the doctor. We're good to go. Still on for tonight?

Oh, yeah. He replied.

I want to come now.

Me too!!!!

He smiled as he texted back.

Don't you dare. Not without me there. I'll make it worth the wait.

I know you will.

He appreciated her confidence in him, her trusting him with her body.

See you soon.

Not soon enough.

CHAPTER THIRTEEN

AFTER HER APPOINTMENT with the doctor, Krissy drove to the plaza across the street for another motherhood first: Perusing sexy undergarments while lugging a six-week-old baby in a car seat.

"Welcome!" A nicely dressed woman with neatly styled blonde hair, maybe in her mid-thirties greeted Krissy as she entered the lingerie store. One look at J.J. and she added, "Let me guess. Gearing up for first time after baby sex?"

Krissy nodded. "First time with the new man in my life sex, too." And not just any man. Spencer. Over the years she'd had a lot of drunk sex, no seduction required. But Spencer was different than the man-boys she typically dated, and she wanted their relationship to be different.

Their relationship.

Thinking that had her feeling euphoric yet frightened at the same time.

"Well then we'll have to find you something

extra special," the saleswoman said with a smile. "Follow me. You breastfeeding?"

Holding the car seat in front of her, Krissy navigated between rack after rack of lacy, silky, sexy outfits. "Yes."

"So we'll need to cover your bra." The saleswoman stopped then looked Krissy over. "I have just the thing."

Seven hours later, dressed in her new sexy lingerie, a silky, deep red outfit sure to drive Spencer wild, Krissy had a bottle of wine chilling, candles out and ready to be lit, and a platter of assorted veggies, crackers, and humus for sustenance, when disaster struck.

"Why tonight? Of all nights?" she asked as she stripped off J.J.'s soiled sleeper. "What did I eat to make this smell so bad?" She undid the tabs of his diaper, taking a moment to mentally prep before opening it. "Good Lord." She held her breath until she couldn't hold it anymore. "The green bean salad I picked up at the deli. Never again."

This mess required more cleansing power than baby wipes. And Spencer, who always came early, would likely be here any minute.

"Oh, well," Krissy told J.J, dropping a kiss on

his forehead. "He'll just have to wait." And so would she.

Wrapping J.J. in a towel she picked him up, walked to the bathroom and set him down on the mat while she readied his bath. No sooner did she put him in the baby bathtub, Spencer knocked on her front door. Knowing he'd worry if she didn't answer, and knowing she couldn't leave J.J. unattended in the tub, she scooped him up, covered him with a towel, and went to the door.

"Sorry," she said when she opened it. "This was not the greeting I'd planned on. You may want to come back in an hour."

Spencer made the mistake of inhaling.

"Appears my afternoon snack didn't agree with the little man here."

Spencer smiled. "You made that big smell?" he asked J.J. "High five." He held out his hand and tapped J.J.'s fist. "Your daddy would be proud."

"Don't encourage him."

"What can I do to help?" Spencer asked.

Unprepared for the sweet offer, Krissy just looked at him, and to her absolute horror, she felt her eyes fill with tears. "I wanted tonight to be special. I bought a negligee." She reached for the bottom hem and held it out so he could see it. "One look at me and you were supposed to go crazy with lust and take me up against the door. Instead, here I am, holding a stinky baby. My new negligee is soaked and quite possibly as stinky as the baby."

She met his eyes again. "This stuff happens when you have a baby. And we're a package deal. So maybe it's a good thing you see what it's like early on so…" If you don't want to be a part of it you can back out now.

Spencer reached out and wiped the tears from beneath her right eye, then her left. "Tonight *will* be special," he said sincerely. "Only a little later than planned. And that sex against the door scenario you had in mind?" He shook his head. "Never would have happened, not tonight anyway. Tonight we're taking it slow. But greet me in that negligee without a stinky baby in your arms, any night after tonight, and you can count on some door pounding action."

The smile came to Krissy's face without her even thinking about it. "Good to know."

"Now what do we have to do to get the little guy settled?" Spencer rubbed his hands together.

"You don't have to—"

"I *want* to."

"Well, he needs a bath and his crib and changing table need to be changed."

Spencer hesitated. "I was thinking more along the lines of me holding him while you handle the smelly stuff."

Krissy gave him a playful shove.

"Hey. I'm new at this. I need to work up to the gross stuff."

Krissy liked that he planned to stick around long enough to work up to the big stuff. "Come on." She walked to the bathroom.

Spencer followed. "I'm glad you're using the baby bathtub."

Krissy dumped out the dirty water and added fresh, warmer water. "Good call. Turned out I needed it after all."

As Krissy washed J.J. Spencer stood behind her, watching, and she didn't mind at all. Early on, she probably would have thought he was critiquing her technique, and he probably would have been. But now, it felt more like he was trying to learn by observing in addition to just keeping them company.

J.J. splashed.

"Wow. He really likes the water."

"Yeah. But it makes giving him a bath a wet undertaking." Krissy glanced over at Spencer. "I wonder if he'll be as good a swimmer as Jarrod?" Jarrod had been a member of their high school swim team.

"Time will tell." Spencer handed her a towel.

She laid it out on the bath mat then lifted a slippery J.J. from the tub, laid him down on it, and swaddled him up.

"Is that the towel I got you?"

Krissy nodded. "Another perfect gift. Thank you." She lifted J.J. and turned to Spencer. "Since you're here to help." She placed J.J. in his arms. "Give me a minute to clean out the tub."

That done, Krissy changed and dressed J.J. out in the living room, leaving him in Spencer's care while she tackled clean up and odor control. "I should have listened when you suggested I get a two bedroom," she yelled down the hall. Then she opened both of her bedroom windows.

When Spencer didn't answer, she went to find out why.

"Shh," he said, holding his fingers to his lips.

He sat leaning back on the couch with J.J. sound asleep on his chest, looking every bit a proud papa. Krissy's heart swelled, knowing deep down in her soul, that no matter what happened between the two of them, Spencer would always play a special role in J.J.'s life.

"I hate to do this, but I need to run the dirty linens down to the laundry room. They're stinking up the whole apartment."

He nodded. "But change first."

She looked down. Right, she was still in her negligee. Her wet, stained, anything but sexy at the moment, negligee. Sixty dollars, wasted. Oh, well, nothing she could do about it now.

When Krissy got back from the laundry room, she found Spencer in her bedroom, leaning over the crib, rubbing J.J.'s back.

When he noticed her watching he pointed at J.J. and gave her a wide-eyed, big-mouthed smile that seemed to say, 'Look what I did!'

"Great job," she whispered giving him two thumbs up. Then she added, "I'm going to take a quick shower."

He nodded.

Her lilac scented body wash smelled so good and the hot water felt so good, Krissy decided to take a little longer than a quick shower to relax and regroup and decide how to restart her seduction. On the verge of shutting off the water, Spencer knocked then opened the door.

"Wanted to run something by you," he said.

Krissy stuck her head out of the side of the shower curtain. "What's up?"

Spencer stared like a man hoping if he tried hard enough he could conjure up X-ray vision. "In my Internet travels I came across articles on breastfeeding women and sex."

Krissy fought a smile. "Oh, you did, did you?"

His eyes finally found hers. "I just want to make it clear that I am perfectly fine with you wearing a bra during sex. But listening to you in the shower gave me an idea."

"Oh, it did, did it?"

He nodded. "Leaky breasts don't matter in the shower, right?"

She liked where this was headed. "No they don't."

"I was hoping you'd say that." He whipped his

polo shirt over his head. "Because I really…" he stared at that shower curtain again "…*really* want to see all of you." He unbuttoned then unzipped his pants. "Feel all of you, bare skin to bare skin while I make love to you, especially this first time." He shucked his pants, underpants and socks. Spencer Penn naked was absolute male perfection. Defined muscles, a light dusting of hair on his chest, and an impressive erection that she couldn't wait to feel inside of her. "So what do you think about slow, careful shower sex?" he asked. "Or start in the shower and finish on the couch sex?"

"I think you put a lot of thought into this."

He nodded. "I put a lot of thought into everything." He bent down, took a condom out of his pants pocket and held it up. "It's an affliction."

"It's not a *bad* thing."

"I'm glad you think so."

"In fact I like a man who puts a lot of thought into things and comes up with ideas like slow, careful, fully naked shower sex." She pulled back the curtain. "Get in here."

Never had a man seemed more eager to join her in a tub. "I was hoping you'd say that." Wasting no time he ripped the packet, rolled on the condom and pulled her into his arms. "God you feel good." He let out a breath. "I feel like I've been waiting a lifetime to hold you like this."

His hands roamed down her back to her butt, he squeezed both cheeks then pulled her close, bending then arching so his erection slid between her legs, front to back. And he began thrusting along her sex.

"That feels so good." Krissy rocked her hips, hoping her legs wouldn't give out. She planted her hands on his butt cheeks, then gave a squeeze and yanked him forward, holding him still so she could glide along his slick length, over and over again.

Spencer moved his arms to her back, squeezed her tight, and pressed her breasts to his chest as he swiveled from side to side. "I knew you'd feel like this. So soft."

A needy pressure built between her legs. Krissy found his nipple and sucked it into her mouth, still rocking.

Spencer sucked in a breath. "Next time I will last longer, I promise."

She sucked again, tilting her pelvis, bringing his tip to her opening.

"You ready?" Spencer asked.

"So ready."

He turned her so she was facing the wall. "Put your leg on the side of the tub." He moved behind her, his front pressed to her back, as he positioned himself at her opening once more. "Talk me in," he said. "Let me know how you feel." He dipped inside.

Suddenly Krissy felt a little nervous.

Somehow Spencer knew.

"It's going to be good." He wrapped an arm around her front, loosely, not restraining her in any way, holding the weight of her right breast in his hand, as he dipped inside a little further.

The sensation familiar and yet different. "More," she said.

He pulled out and slid back in, deeper. Krissy's body stretched to accommodate him. "Again."

He pulled out and pushed forward.

This time Krissy pushed back, taking more of him.

Spencer sucked in a shuddery breath. "God how

you test me." He pulled her close and started to move, gently, slowly.

Krissy moved with him, the rhythm perfect. Until she needed, "More."

He gave her more of him until she took all of him.

"Faster."

He picked up the pace, his breath turning into a pant by her ear.

"Harder."

"You're sure?"

"I'm sure."

He slammed into her from behind, over and over, caressing both of her breasts now, squeezing them, while avoiding her tender nipples, as if he somehow knew.

"You feel so good inside of me," she told him, meeting each powerful thrust with one of her own. "I need your hand." She removed it from her breast. "Here." She placed it between her legs, didn't need to do anything more than that because it was like he knew exactly what to do.

"God you're good at this." He possessed her, controlled her, used her body, taking what he wanted, but giving so much more. Her orgasm started to build. "Please tell me you're close."

"Ready when you are," he panted in her ear, driving into her from behind, fondling her from the front, replacing the memory of every man before him with the memory of what he was doing to her right now.

"Now," she said, straining out her release. "Now." She came again.

Spencer let out a grunt and stiffened against her back. He pulled out, thrust in deep and held himself there, grunting again, kissing her ear, her neck, hugging her tightly. "I want to stay like this for the rest of the night."

"Not sure the hot water will hold out."

"Too bad."

Too bad indeed.

Krissy lowered her leg and Spencer left her body. She felt the loss of their connection immediately, missing it, wanting it again. Turning she threw her arms around his neck and pulled him down for a kiss.

He kissed her over and over, affectionate and caring kisses turning passionate. "That was so good. Just like I knew it would be." He turned off the water, reached for the towel on the hook, and wrapped her in it. "How do you feel?" He looked deep into her eyes as if trying to ascertain the truth there.

Krissy climbed out of the tub, reached inside the cabinet beneath the sink, and handed him a fresh towel. "I feel wonderful," she told him the truth, stretching. "I wish…"

"What?"

"My place isn't set up very well for entertaining men."

In the process of towel drying his head, he stopped and looked at her. "Good."

"Whoa." She held up both hands. "Down boy. I only meant, I have a twin-sized bed in a bedroom that I share with my baby. My couch doesn't open into a sleeper—" He started to speak. She held up a finger to stop him and kept talking, "which in hindsight may have been a mistake. Yes I probably should have listened to you. What I was trying to say, before you went jealous male on me," which she kind of liked, "is that I don't have any place where we can lie down together. Comfortably." To cuddle.

Spencer pulled her into his arms. "From now on, we'll use my place. I've got a nice big bed.

We can get one of those portable cribs and set it up in the living room for J.J."

"Always thinking." She smiled. "I like that."

"As for tonight." He kissed the top of her head. "The couch is fine. When I get tired I'll head back to my place."

CHAPTER FOURTEEN

OVER THE NEXT few weeks, Krissy began spending more nights in Spencer's bed than in her own. His orderly apartment had turned disorderly. Baby stuff cluttered his living room, dishes sat in his sink, unwashed, and dirty clothes and towels seemed to materialize out of nowhere, draped on his couch, balled on his bathroom floor, and piled in the corner of his bedroom. And he didn't mind one bit.

It amazed him how quickly he'd transitioned from happily single bachelor to contented family man, how easily he'd fallen into the role of dad for J.J., and how much he'd grown to care for Krissy, in such a short time. She didn't nag, or complain, or question where he'd been or where he was going. She didn't call him throughout the day, didn't demand his attention, and really didn't seem to expect anything from him. She was smart and sexy, fun and most importantly, independent. She was the perfect woman.

He recalled a snippet from Jarrod's letter.

Look at her. Really look. Past her pretty face and hot body, beyond her flirty behavior and sarcasm, deeper, to the sweet, thoughtful, special woman she is inside.

In the last few weeks, Spencer had done just that. And it hadn't taken him long to realize how lucky he was to have Krissy in his life. He looked to the corner of his sofa where he had J.J. propped up beside him. "What do you think of the game, buddy?" Spencer pointed to his laptop screen where 'they' were watching NYC United play the Arizona Wolfpack, in Arizona.

J.J. smiled at the attention and shook his rattle.

During halftime Spencer called to Krissy who was in the kitchen preparing a lasagna for dinner. "How are you feeling about Patti and Bart's big news?" Their plans to relocate up to White Plains to be closer to Krissy and J.J.

"I'm actually looking forward to it." She walked out of the kitchen, drying her hands on a towel, and came to sit beside him on the couch. "I'm anxious to get back to work. With Patti willing to babysit J.J., it's the perfect situation for me. I think having them close will be good for all of us."

Spencer thought so, too, couldn't wait to have access to local babysitters he trusted so he could take Krissy out on dates and they could spend more time doing 'couple' things. "My friend Steve asked if we'd like to go out for dinner with him and his wife on Wednesday. She's six months pregnant, and they're fine with us bringing J.J." It'd be their first time taking J.J. out to a restaurant. Heck, it'd be Spencer's first time taking Krissy out to a restaurant.

"Wednesday doesn't work for me."

What? What did she mean Wednesday didn't work for her? He waited for her to explain. She didn't. So he asked, "You have other plans?" With who?

She stared back at him but said nothing.

"With J.J.?"

"Nah, I think I'll leave the kid home alone. He can't walk or crawl yet, what trouble can he get into?" J.J. started to fuss so Krissy walked over to pick him up. "Of course, with J.J. I'm breast-feeding. I do everything with J.J. I go everywhere with J.J. He is always with me, twenty-four hours a day, seven days a week!"

"I'm sorry. Of course you'll be with J.J. Stupid question." Spencer moved the laptop from his lap to the coffee table. "So where are you going?" As long as Spencer wasn't traveling they spent every evening and most nights together. Exactly what plans did Krissy have that didn't include him?

She swayed on her feet, rocking J.J. while rubbing his back, appearing not at all eager to tell him.

Which made him want to know even more. "What's the big secret? Why won't you tell me where you're going on Wednesday?"

"It's no big deal and I don't want you worrying that—" She stopped mid-sentence.

"Don't want me worrying about what?" He sat up straighter.

"I knew you'd make a big deal about it, so I didn't plan to tell you until after I did it."

"Did what?"

Never one to back down, her eyes met his. "Introduce J.J. to my mom."

Her brain-injured mother who Spencer hadn't seen since her injury, but who he'd heard plenty of stories about back in the day. "Your mother? Who has violent outbursts?" At least she used to. "Who doesn't even know who you are? Why would you put J.J. at risk to meet a woman who doesn't even know who you are?"

"Wow. That was a jerky thing to say." Krissy walked over to J.J.'s diaper bag, picked it up and set it on the recliner. Then she started walking around the living room collecting J.J.'s things one handed. "Regardless of whether she remembers who I am or not, she's still my mother." Krissy wouldn't look at him. "*I* remember her the way she used to be, before the brain injury turned her into a different person. *I* want to introduce her to *my* son, not because it will mean something to her, but because it'll mean something to *me*."

He'd hurt her feelings, the very last thing he'd wanted to do. "I'm sorry."

"You should be sorry." She bent down to pick up J.J.'s blanket from the portable crib, balancing J.J. on her hip at the same time.

"Let me help you."

Before he could reach her, she whipped up the blanket, nearly toppling the crib over. "I don't need your help."

"Stop." He grabbed her by the shoulders, turning her around so she had to look at him. "I'm sorry. Of course you should take J.J. to meet your mother. I'll go with you." To ensure his godson's safety.

Krissy looked mortified at the thought. "You can't."

He can't? "Oh, yes, I can," Spencer said. "And to keep J.J. safe, I will."

Krissy looked ready to lash out at him, but she didn't. Instead she inhaled then exhaled and said, "I'm going to ignore your overbearing statement, because I know you said it with J.J.'s best interest at heart. But to clarify, *no*, you *can't* go with us. We won't be alone. Kira and Derrick will be there. We'll all make sure J.J. is safe."

"You'd rather have Kira and Derrick there than me? I have no say? After all I've done for you?"

Krissy went rigid. "After all you've done for me?"

"Taking you to Lamaze class."

"You mean forcing me to go to Lamaze class."

He ignored that comment. They both knew she had to go. "Being with you in the delivery room, buying you things." He ticked the items off on his fingers, one by one. "Bringing you dinner, helping you with J.J., spending all of my free time with you, changing my whole life for you." The moment the last word left his mouth, Spencer knew he'd gone too far.

"Well. Tell me how you really feel," Krissy said calmly, way too calmly. He would have preferred it if she'd blown up at him.

"Right or wrong, that *is* how I feel," Spencer said. "We're close enough and I do enough for you that I feel I deserve a say in you bringing J.J. into an unsafe situation. And if I want to be there, I believe I have earned the right to be there."

"You believe you have earned the right?" Krissy glared at him. "Let's get something straight," she said her stance rigid and ready for battle. "J.J. is *my* son. *Mine*, not yours. If I want to take him to meet my mother, I will take him to meet my mother. While I appreciate everything you have done for me, I didn't realize you were under the mistaken impression your actions entitled you to certain rights where *my* son is concerned." She shoved J.J.'s rattle, a burping cloth, and a stuffy into the diaper bag.

"Out of respect and appreciation," she snapped,

in a tone that didn't sound respectful or apprecia-tive, "I will explain that since my mother's attack she has developed a severe fear of men. All men. Age, hair color, ethnicity, none of it matters. If a male comes near her she reacts. If she feels threat-ened, she flies into a rage and goes on the attack. Other times, like if she hears a male voice, it could even be on the television if she's not right in front of the screen, she'll bang her head on the closest hard surface until it bleeds. Or she'll stab herself with a sharp object, over and over until we can get it away from her. It's not something I talk about. Now you know. The reason you *can't* come with me to visit my mother, is because you're a man. It's not safe for you and it's not safe for her."

"So why does Derrick get to go?" Jeez. Even to his own ears he sounded like a spoiled child.

"Because he dresses like a woman, that's why."

"He dresses like a woman? That's the most ri-diculous thing I've ever heard."

Krissy glared at him, again. "Yes. He dresses like a woman, so he can spend time with Kira while she's taking care of my mom, so he can help her and provide medical evaluation and treatment when Mom needs it." She pointed her finger in his direction. "If you tell anyone or tease him or say one unkind word to him about it, I will never forgive you. He's a great guy." Apparently talking about Derrick calmed her down. "He loves Kira, would do anything for her. She is blessed to have a man like him in her life." She hefted the diaper bag and slung the strap over her shoulder.

"Don't go," he tried.

"I don't want to intrude on your free time," Krissy said. "Your dinner is in the oven. Timer is set."

"Krissy…"

She reached for her pocketbook which hung on the back of a kitchen chair. The heavy diaper bag slid down her arm, throwing her off balance.

"Let me help you." Spencer reached for the diaper bag.

"Don't." She twisted out of reach. "Now that I know your help comes with expectations, I won't be so willing to accept it in the future." She turned to walk toward the door. "I knew you were like Kira, I just didn't recognize how much until today."

She said it like it was a bad thing. "What's that supposed to mean?"

"It means you do things for me, things I don't ask for, then, when you get mad at me, you throw them back in my face. If you didn't want to spend so much time with me, you shouldn't have. If you didn't want to buy things for me and J.J., you shouldn't have. If you didn't want to attend J.J.'s birth or drive us to Patti and Bart's, you shouldn't have." She opened the door then turned to look at him. "And for the record, no one asked you to change your life for me."

In the heat of the moment, "That's not exactly true," shot out of his mouth.

Krissy turned, slowly. "What did you say?"

Spencer regretted his words instantly and did not want to repeat them.

Krissy stood there, staring laser beams of rage in his direction.

Everything inside of him screamed now was not the time to tell her, that he should wait to explain after they'd both had a chance to calm down.

"Tell me," Krissy demanded. "You've got something to say, say it. Let's get everything out in the open, right here, right now."

At this point he'd do anything to be done with this fight, so they could talk it out and move on.

So he told her the truth. "In his letter," Spencer explained. "Jarrod asked me to help you with J.J. To help you raise J.J."

Her eyes met his. "Jarrod didn't trust me to do it on my own?" Anger turned to hurt. She curled a protective arm around J.J. "He didn't think I'd be a good mother? That's the only reason you…" Anger flared back to life. "That's the only reason you've been so nice to me? To worm your way into my life, so you can help raise J.J., because Jarrod asked you to?"

"No—"

"How could I have been so stupid to think you actually cared about me?"

"Krissy—"

"Well at least you got some great sex out of it, right? If you have to change your life for a woman you hate, and pretend to like her and care for her baby, because your dead friend asked you to, at the very least you deserve lots of great sex…as payment for all you've sacrificed."

"I didn't—"

"Don't you dare say you didn't enjoy it," she yelled. "I am one hundred percent certain you were at least happy to have me in your bed, and that you enjoyed yourself as much and as often as I did." Her eyes met his, full of challenge. "If you say otherwise you're a liar."

Spencer's nosy neighbor across the hall opened her door and stuck her head out.

"Come back inside," Spencer said calmly as he walked toward Krissy. "Let me explain."

"There's nothing to explain. Jarrod trusted me to give birth to his baby but not to raise it. So he sicced *you* on me, and you took full advantage of that." J.J. started to cry. Krissy bounced him in her arms as she fired off her parting shots. "As of today I am officially done with you. Stay away from me. Don't try to talk to me. Don't look in my direction. Don't even think about me. As of this very second, you are as dead to me as Jarrod is."

With that she turned and stormed away.

Spencer let her go. He had no choice. She was so upset, there was no way they could have a rational conversation. With a nod to his neighbor he closed his door. He'd give Krissy a few hours to calm down. Then he'd go to her apartment to apologize…and tell her the whole truth.

CHAPTER FIFTEEN

KRISSY FLED SPENCER'S APARTMENT, his building, and his life. Then she loaded J.J. into his car seat in her car and drove. "How could I have been so stupid? To actually believe he cared about me?" Needing to hit something she pounded on the steering wheel at each slow moving vehicle in her way, each red traffic light that delayed her escape. She needed speed, needed to get away.

Of course she'd known their relationship would end at some point, but tonight's revelations had come out of nowhere, everything had been going so well. Or so she'd thought.

Jarrod didn't trust you, after all.

Spencer didn't trust you, either.

Krissy sucked in a breath. What about Patti and Bart? What had Jarrod written in his letter to them? Is that why they were moving to White Plains? To be closer to Krissy so they could check up on her, too? Because they didn't trust her with J.J. either?

Krissy's chest burned with hurt.

As if he could tell something was very wrong, J.J. started to cry. "It's okay, baby." But it wasn't okay. Nothing was okay.

And yet, as angry and hurt as she was, she slowed the car, knew she shouldn't be driving reckless. She was a mother now, a good, responsible mother, no matter what anyone else thought. Rather than flying into a rage or running away, she needed to find a way to *make* things okay, for herself and her son, starting with getting out of the car so she could dry his tears and hug him close and reassure him that he was safe and loved.

"A few more minutes, honey. Just give me a few more minutes."

Not wanting to return to her apartment ever again, and having no place else to go, she drove to Kira's.

Later that night, laying on a new twin bed in the extra room at Kira's house, alone in the dark, Krissy listened and watched the light on the baby monitor for any movement. Only in her second trimester of pregnancy, ever efficient, ever prepared Kira already had her nursery partially set up. So it made sense to put J.J. to sleep there, at least to Kira. But Krissy missed having him close, no longer liked being alone.

When she heard the front door to Kira's house open, she forced herself to sit up and wipe her annoyingly weepy eyes, then she forced herself to stand and walk and act like her world hadn't fallen apart this evening. "Hey," she said to Kira who was walking up the stairs, carrying bags of stuff she'd gone to get from Krissy's apartment, even though Krissy had insisted it could wait until tomorrow. "Need help?" Without waiting for an answer, she met Kira halfway and took the bags from her right hand.

"Feeling better?" Kira asked.

"Yes," she lied. "Thank you so much for letting J.J. and me stay here for a little while and for getting my stuff. I won't stay long, I promise." Just long enough to figure out her next move.

"Stay as long as you want," Kira said, planting a kiss on Krissy's cheek as she walked past. "I need to use the bathroom."

From behind Kira, on the stairs, carrying the baby bath, the bouncy chair J.J. loved, and more bags of stuff from her apartment, Derrick said, "Don't think you have to leave because of me. Kira's family is my family." Kira had hit the future husband jackpot with that man, a keeper for sure.

"Thank you." When Derrick put down his bundles, Krissy went over to give him a hug. "At least I know J.J. will always have you to look up to and learn from." She hugged him tighter.

Derrick hugged her back. "I am going to be the best uncle in the history of uncles."

See, she didn't need Spencer. J.J. was going to grow up just fine. Krissy was going to be just fine too…as soon as the ache in her heart went away.

"I'm making tea," Kira said, joining them in the foyer. "Anyone else want?"

Derrick walked over to Kira and put his arm around her shoulders, but he spoke to Krissy. "She drinks tea before bed then complains when she has to get up in the middle of the night to pee."

Kira smiled up at him. "Sometimes you like it when I wake up in the middle of the night to pee."

Derrick gave her a very sexy smile back. "Sometimes I do." He kissed her.

There was so much love between the two of them. Despite her heartache, Krissy couldn't help feeling happy for her sister. No one deserved the love of a good man more than Kira.

"I've got an early day tomorrow," Derrick said. "I'm going to bed."

After another loving kiss for his fiancée, he headed down the hall.

"Come sit with me," Kira said, walking back into the kitchen. "Since you've been seeing Spencer, we haven't had much sister time."

Sister time sounded perfect, so Krissy pulled out a chair and took a seat at the counter. "As long as you know I'm still not ready to talk about what happened tonight." Aside from the humiliation of learning Jarrod hadn't trusted her to raise his son on her own and Spencer's actions had been motivated by an obligation to his friend and lust, rather than any real care for her, this was Krissy's problem, Krissy's life. And she'd deal with it on her own.

"That's fine," Kira said, carrying her mug of tea to the counter and sitting next to Krissy.

"What?" Krissy eyed her sister. "That's fine?" She hit the side of her head trying to clear a fake blockage from her ear canals. "Did you say that's fine?" She studied Kira's face, staring into her eyes, looking… "You must be an alien impos-ter," Krissy said. "Because my *real* sister would be questioning me and analyzing the information provided and telling me what I should do."

Kira smiled. "Derrick lectured me all the way home from your apartment." She dropped her voice to mimic him. "She has to fix this on her own, Kira. You can't solve all of her problems, Kira. She's a grown woman, Kira."

Yes, she was. "Have I mentioned how much I love my soon-to-be brother-in-law?"

"You and everyone else," Kira said. "While he's not always right, I think in this instance he is." She reached out and squeezed Krissy's hand. "Just know I'm here for you. I'm here to listen when you're ready to talk, to be a sounding board, if you want one, to give my opinion if, and only if you ask for it. I'll babysit. I'll pack up your apartment and move all of your things wherever you tell me to move them. I'll act as intermediary between you and Spencer so he can play a role in J.J.'s life, if that's what he wants, without you ever having to speak to him again, not that I think that's the best course of action, but it doesn't matter what

254 THE NURSE'S NEWBORN GIFT

I think. The decision of what path your life will take from here is all yours and yours alone."

With Kira's words fresh in her mind, the first major decision Krissy made was to cancel on Sunday dinner at Patti and Bart's. She felt awful about that, especially since she'd been the one to suggest starting them up again. But she wasn't ready to see any of them.

The following week, Patti called to say Spencer wouldn't be joining them for Sunday dinner and offer Bart's services to drive her and J.J. into and home from the city. Wanting to talk to them alone, Krissy agreed to dinner, but declined the offer of transportation. She was fully capable of driving herself into the city. And on Sunday, she made the trip without any problems. J.J. slept, traffic moved, she found a great parking spot close by, and actually wound up arriving twenty minutes early. Bart met her down in the main floor entryway so she didn't have to carry J.J. and the diaper bag up the stairs.

"Look at that big boy," Bart said as he hurried down the stairs. "He looks like he's doubled in size since I last saw him."

It'd only been two weeks, and they'd Skyped

twice since then. "Thanks for coming down to get him." Krissy lifted J.J. out of the carrier she wore draped across her front and handed him to Bart. "Go to Grandpa."

Recognizing his grandpa, J.J.'s legs started to pump with glee.

"He's smiling." Which made Bart smile too.

"He's been doing that a lot lately." So had Krissy, she was moving on with her life and things were going well.

Up in the apartment, Patti greeted her as warmly as ever. "I'm so happy you came." She gave Krissy a tight hug. "How was your trip?"

"Not bad at all." Krissy set her bags on the floor then maneuvered out of the baby carrier. "But the downside of me coming by myself, is I didn't have enough hands to bring dessert."

"I know you like fruit salad," Spencer said from the doorway into the kitchen. "So I brought some. No bananas or strawberries."

Spencer.

He looked so good in his dark blue jeans and blue and white striped polo shirt. But Krissy forced her eyes away, turning to Patti who now held J.J. "You told me Spencer wasn't coming."

Spencer answered. "If you knew I'd be here, you wouldn't have come."

True.

"We need to talk," Spencer said.

Krissy looked from Spencer to Patti to Bart, who had conveniently positioned himself between her and door. "So you're all in on this." They were ganging up on her, and Patti and Bart had taken Spencer's side, which made it clear, whatever concerns Jarrod had shared with Spencer, he'd also shared with his parents.

"We're not taking sides," Patti said. "We're simply watching J.J. so the two of you can talk out your problems uninterrupted."

Spencer walked toward her, looking so serious, so weary. "Give me fifteen minutes. If you want me to go after that, I'll leave."

Figuring the sooner he said what he'd come here to say, the sooner he'd leave, Krissy agreed. "Okay."

Looking relieved, Patti, who was still holding J.J., turned to follow Bart, who carried the diaper bag, down the hall to their bedroom. The door clicked closed behind her.

Spencer took a seat at the kitchen table.

Krissy grabbed a glass and filled it with water then she sat too.

"I've given this a lot of thought." Spencer held out an envelope labeled with his name in Jarrod's handwriting. "I want you to read the letter Jarrod left for me."

Krissy reached for it.

Spencer held it tight. "First, you have to promise to read it through from start to finish without getting angry or upset or asking questions. Second, after you're done reading, you have to agree to keep quiet and give me a full ten minutes to explain."

His expression dire, Krissy wasn't sure she wanted to read it. But curiosity got the better of her, and she nodded. "I promise and I agree."

With suddenly sweaty hands, she opened the envelope, took out the letter, and started to read.

Hey Spence,

If you're reading this, I guess I zigged when I should have zagged and I'm dead. Well, doesn't that suck? I hope I went out in a blaze of glory doing something heroic.

I know we're on shaky terms right now because you don't agree with my reason for join-

ing the Army. But it's my decision, my life. And if my plan works, and Krissy and I wind up together, well, it'll be a happy life indeed. Sure, I'm not a fan of getting blown up in some foreign country, but if I do what I've been trained to do, I should be fine. Anyway, in the States, I could get killed simply crossing the street, right? No honor in that.

Now for the important stuff. If I know Krissy—and I know her better than anyone— she's probably waited until the last possible minute to give you this letter. So by now you can probably tell she's pregnant. Surprise! The baby is mine. I wish I could see her belly rounded with my child, wish I could be there to run to the store to buy stuff to satisfy her crazy cravings and hold her hand through labor and help her care for and raise our child. But obviously I can't.

In my absence, Krissy will try to do everything on her own, but she can't. She'll need help. And I expect you, my oldest and best friend, my blood brother since the third grade, to be there for her. That's why I made you the baby's godfather.

You're the best guy I know, Spence. I trust you to help Krissy raise my son or daughter the way I would have. Not because I don't think she's going to be a fantastic mother—because I know, without a doubt, she's going to be a fantastic mother. And not because I don't think she'll raise my child right—because I know she will. But I don't want her to have to do it alone. I don't want her to struggle and sacrifice, like so many single mothers do.

I know you had a crush on her at one point. I saw the way you used to look at her when you thought no one would notice, like you wanted to strip her bare and get down to business on the closest flat surface. Yet you never acted on that urge, at least as far as I know, out of respect for me, I'm sure. Another reason you're the best guy I know. Maybe I should have bowed out. I'm pretty sure she had a thing for you for a while, too. I'm selfish enough to admit, I liked it better when the two of you were fighting than when you were lusting after each other.

But things have changed. With me no lon-

ger in the picture, there's no one I'd rather Krissy be with more than you. I know you'll treat her the way she deserves to be treated.

If she's not in a relationship, or the guy she's with is her typical A-hole of a boyfriend, and if you're not in a serious relationship, I want you to turn on the charm and win her over. Dig deep. Remember how you used to feel about her before you two started fighting, re-ignite that old spark. Be nice. Be helpful. Be there when she needs you.

You were always so quick to see the bad in Krissy. Well, I got news for you, buddy. No one's perfect. Get over the past. Look at her. Really look. Past her pretty face and hot body, beyond her flirty behavior and sarcasm, deeper, to the sweet, thoughtful, special woman she is inside. Honest to God, I am giving you a gift, the life I always wanted for myself, a fun, loving woman who, if you let her, will make you happy. I know she will.

Wish I could be there when Krissy tells my mom and dad that they're grandparents. I get choked up thinking about it. Anyway, I

*know you'll do the right thing. Even so, I'll
be watching.*
Love you, man,
Jarrod
So Jarrod *had* trusted her.

*…because I know, without a doubt, she's
going to be a fantastic mother.*

Krissy's heart swelled with love. Then it de-
flated with loss because Jarrod wasn't here. Only
Spencer was here—Spencer, who had only been
a part of her life because Jarrod had asked him to
be, guilted him to be.

*And I expect you, my oldest and best friend,
my blood brother since the third grade, to be
there for her.*

Krissy's eyes met Spencer's. "If you expected
this letter to help your case, it didn't. Nice to know
you're always so quick to see the bad in me."

"So much for you agreeing to keep quiet and
give me a chance to explain."

Krissy crossed her arms over her chest, braced
herself for what he was about to say, and glanced
at the clock on the microwave. "Your ten minutes
starts now."

CHAPTER SIXTEEN

KRISSY SAT ACROSS from Spencer, looking hurt and ready to hurl her water glass at his head at the same time. Letting her read Jarrod's letter had been a risk. But if they were to have any chance for a future together, there could be no secrets between them.

"To start," Spencer said. "The last time I saw you I acted like a total jerk."

"An adequate description." She nodded as if giving it further consideration. "A decent place to start."

"I'm sorry."

Her posture softened considerably.

"I need you to know that I wasn't being nice or helpful simply to get you into bed." He stared deeply into her eyes. "You have to believe me."

She stared back, but said nothing.

Not good.

"Sex with you has me thinking words like transcendent and unrivaled and unsurpassable. And let's face it, those aren't words I use on a regular basis."

She gifted him with a small smile. "I like those words."

He did too. "Why do you think that is?"

"We've got some crazy sexual chemistry going on."

"No." He reached over to take her hand into his. "It's because what's between us is deeper and more meaningful than just sex. My need for you is so much more powerful than simple sexual attraction. Regardless of what brought us together, I've come to care for you, Krissy."

She shook her head and tried to pull her hand away.

He held on tight, wouldn't let her go until he said all he'd come here to say. "Yes, in the beginning I got involved with you because Jarrod had asked me to."

"And probably because you thought I'd be a total screw-up of a mother."

Seeing her hurt made him hurt. "Back when you first showed up at my door, I'd had no idea you'd grown up to be such a responsible, committed, and capable woman."

Her eyes met his. "Thank you, Spencer. That means a lot."

"I helped you because it was the right thing to do, because you needed my help. But honest to God, I enjoyed spending time with you. Which is why, even after I assured myself you were a wonderful mother and you were taking great care of J.J. and really didn't need anything from me, I kept on stopping by. Because I *wanted* to, not because I felt I *needed* to. Because I started to care for you…again."

"Did you really have a crush on me back in high school?" She tilted her head. "You sure had an odd way of showing it." She seemed to give it some thought. "Because of Jarrod."

He nodded. "He'd been so in love with you for so long. I couldn't…"

Krissy squeezed his hand. "You're a great friend, Spencer."

Sometimes he didn't feel like one.

"But even so," she went on. "You shouldn't be expected to change your life, to take on responsibility for a woman and her baby, simply because your friend asked you to. Jarrod was wrong to—"

"No, he wasn't," Spencer insisted. "I'm glad he

asked. I know I didn't sound like it, but I'm happy having you and J.J. as part of my life. I know I'm not his father and I had no right to—"

"I was wrong," Krissy interrupted.

What? "No."

"Hear me out," Krissy said. "I've given this a lot of thought. When we started sleeping together, I treated our relationship like I've treated every other sexual relationship I've had. I guarded my heart so you wouldn't break it, and I made sure to remain independent so that when whatever this is between us runs its course and we break up, I'll be just fine getting back to life on my own."

Spencer tried to say something but Krissy shushed him.

"My point is, you were right. You'd taken on a fatherly role for J.J. and I let you. It's obvious to me that you love him as if he were your own son."

"I do."

"So like I said, I was wrong to make the decision to go see my mom, knowing the risks involved, without discussing it with you first. Even though you're not technically J.J.'s father, you're the closest thing he has to one."

"Thank you. And I was wrong for throwing

everything I've done for you back in your face, like Kira does. I was *happy* to go with you to Lamaze class, I *wanted* to be in the delivery room, and aside from leaky, smelly diapers and getting woken up in the middle of the night, I love everything else about being with you and J.J."

"You do take good care of us, just like Jarrod had asked you to."

Spencer's heart swelled with joy and pride and hope. "Thank you."

"So where do we go from here?" Krissy asked, avoiding contact.

"I'm hoping we can try again," Spencer told her.

She lifted her eyes to meet his. "I'd like that, too."

Thank you, God.

"But from today on, things need to change."

He didn't want things to change, liked them just the way they were.

"Don't look so worried," she smiled. "I mean change as in we need to do things the right way this time. Go out on dates, just the two of us. Get to know each other again. Have fun. Go out with friends, together or alone. Have lives that aren't dependent on one another. Create a relationship based on more than taking care of J.J. and having great sex."

He liked the sound of that.

"No more spending all of our free time together. One thing I've realized in our time apart is that I need to find a balance between me the mom and me the fun-loving woman I was before I became a mom. I need to make new friends and find things to do in my new hometown, which I've already started doing, by the way."

"I saw you've been spending time at an exercise studio on Maple Street."

"I'm taking a Mommy and Me class. We line all the car seats along the back wall. It's the cutest thing." She stiffened.

Uh-oh.

"How did you know I was spending time at an exercise studio on Maple Street?"

He could have tried to lie. Maybe something like, "I saw your car in the parking lot." But no, a future built on no secrets between them meant no secrets between them. He reached into his pocket, took out his cell phone, and accessed his Find Friends app. Then he turned the screen to her.

"Find Friends?"

"It's an app. I loaded it onto your phone."

"At the hospital."

He nodded.

"You've been tracking me?" This time when she pulled her hand away he let her.

He nodded again, waited for her to let him have it, felt everything slipping away. He'd lose her now for sure.

Surprisingly she didn't let him have it. All she did was ask, "Why?"

"I'd told you I would respect your privacy and not visit you without an invitation. I loaded the app so I could keep my distance but still see what you were up to."

Leaning back in her chair, she crossed her arms over her chest. "To make sure I wasn't going out drinking and partying all night?"

"No," he answered, staring her straight in the eyes, showing her he wasn't lying. It hadn't taken long for Spencer to realize how badly he'd misjudged her early on, and to know she was going to be a wonderful mother. "So I could feel close to you, without actually being close to you." He told her the truth. "If that makes any sense at all."

"So you know I've been staying with Kira for the last two weeks."

He nodded again. "Had you been alone in your apartment, I wouldn't have waited until today to try to talk to you."

Rather than yell and carry on like old Krissy would have, she sat calmly and quietly as if digesting all she'd just heard.

Spencer wouldn't allow himself to hope.

By the time she finally spoke, he'd been fully prepared to throw himself to the floor at her feet to beg for forgiveness.

Of all the things to come out of her mouth, "Thank you," the two words in that exact order, were the absolute last two words he'd expected to hear.

Had he misunderstood? "You're thanking me for spying on you?"

Her eyes met his. "I'm thanking you for telling me the truth."

The tightness in Spencer's chest loosened enough for him to take a deep breath. "I'll delete the app."

"Good idea."

He deleted the app. "And since I'm coming clean about my bad behavior…"

"Lord, help me." She shifted in her seat. "You mean there's more?"

"Might as well get it all out now, right? So we can start over with a clean slate."

"Why do I feel like I need a shot of something whiskey-like before you go on?"

"About that kiss in high school," he said.

She let out a relieved breath. "You pushed me away because of Jarrod."

"Yeah. And I got mean and obnoxious to keep you away."

Her lips curved into a small smile. "Or I might have tried again."

"When you wanted something, you were pretty persistent."

"And I'd wanted you."

"For the record, I'd wanted you too. If not for Jarrod, I would have claimed you as mine that night."

She stood. "How about claiming me as yours right now?" She straddled his lap.

Overcome with relief and gratitude, hope and happiness, Spencer threw his arms around her and kissed her like the world might end if he didn't do it thoroughly enough, prepared to sit there, holding her until the end of time.

She held him just as tightly, and kissed him back with equal enthusiasm, his perfect match in every way. So he eased back, to tell her, "You are what my life's been missing. You're fun and passionate, a wonderful mother, and thank God, kind and forgiving. You're laid back, you go with the flow and I need that in my life."

She countered with, "You're confident and sexy, dependable and smart, and you're going to make a wonderful father for J.J., I mean for as long as..." She broke eye contact, looking unsure.

"I'm going to make a wonderful father for J.J. period. End of statement."

"About my mother," Krissy started. "I want my children to know her, even though she showed little interest in J.J. when we brought him over."

He'd been wondering about that. "I handled that all wrong. Of course you should take J.J. to visit her, anytime you want. I trust you to keep him safe. But if you want me to, I will happily dress up like a woman to go with you, not for safety, but to keep you company when you visit or have to care for her. I'd do anything for you, Krissy. And I hope that one day, you'll feel blessed to have me in your life, same as you feel Kira is blessed to have Derrick in hers."

Taking his face in her hands and staring deeply into his eyes she said, "Baby, I already do."

EPILOGUE

Ten years later

KRISSY ENDED HER call just as Patti walked into the kitchen of the house she and Spencer had been living in for the past nine years, since right after they'd gotten married in a double ceremony with Kira and Derrick.

"The boys will be home in ten minutes," Patti said.

Krissy held up her cell phone. "I heard you talking to Bart. I called Kira. She'll be here with all the kids in half an hour." That would give J.J. time to open his two very special presents without the craziness of having his younger brother and sister, and Kira's two children running all around, wanting to see.

Krissy glanced at the letter from Jarrod and the velvet box from Patti and Bart that she'd set on the counter, trying to contain her emotions.

Patti opened the refrigerator door, drawing her attention, and once again, Krissy could not believe her eyes. "You outdid yourself this year." The race car cake Patti had created for J.J.'s tenth birthday celebration looked so realistic, Krissy hated the thought of cutting into it.

"Have to admit," Patti said as she took the cake and carried it to the center of their huge dining room table. "I had to do a few trial runs to get it just right. The people at Bart's work were happy to help us get rid of the duds."

This year J.J. hadn't wanted a big party. He'd only wanted two things, the letter from his dad up in heaven and to indulge his love of NASCAR and attend a race. For as much as J.J.'s looks and mannerisms, and his kind heart, were similar to Jarrod's, their son was most certainly his own person. His obsession with all things auto racing had caught everyone by surprise. But his very involved Grandpa Bart and his loving father here on earth, Spencer, had embraced his love of NASCAR, and went on to develop their own obsessions with it.

Ten minutes flew by in a blur of putting out drinks and food. Before Krissy knew it, the dog started in with his over-the-top happy 'My family is home' barking. A few seconds later J.J. ran into the kitchen to hug his grandma and then Krissy. "We had the best time, Mom."

Bart and Spencer followed, more slowly and lacking J.J.'s energy.

Krissy kissed Spencer's cheek. "An annual event?" she whispered.

"God, I hope not." He hugged her close. "I'm exhausted." They'd left at dawn and it was nearing seven o'clock in the evening. Thank goodness tomorrow Spencer had a day off from his work with NYC United, where he was now the head athletic trainer, so both he and J.J. could spend all of Sunday relaxing.

"Poor baby." Krissy went up on her tiptoes as she pulled him down so she could whisper in his ear. "I missed you today." Nine years of marriage and despite their crazy hectic lives, she loved him now more than ever. "I was hoping to show you how much."

He nuzzled next to her ear. "I'm never too tired for that."

A fact he'd proven time and time again.

"Can I open them now?" J.J. asked.

Krissy, Spencer, Patti and Bart all looked over to where he stood, holding the letter in one hand and the box in the other. The mood in the room instantly changed. J.J.'s excitement was almost palpable. But for Krissy, and she'd guess everyone else, this moment brought back Jarrod's loss once again. His son finally reading the letter he'd left for him would be bittersweet.

"What?" J.J. asked, with a look of frustration that so closely resembled a look Krissy had seen on Jarrod's face way too many times. "I took off my shoes and washed my hands and gave Grandpa Bart time to go to the bathroom."

Grandpa Bart laughed. "That he did."

Krissy smiled. The mood in the room seemed to lighten.

"Which one should I open first?" J.J. asked, eyeing the box then the envelope, trying to decide.

Bart stepped forward and pointed to the velvet box. "I think this one."

Without question, J.J. set down the letter and lifted the top of the box. As he studied the contents he looked confused, maybe a little disappointed even, until Bart explained, "This is your daddy's Congressional Medal of Honor. It was awarded by the President of the United States. It's the highest and most prestigious honor given by the U.S. Military, for extreme acts of bravery and courage."

"Wow," J.J. said with awe and a good amount of reverence. He'd been told the story of how his father had died during a hostage rescue mission when he'd remained behind to lay down cover fire, saving his team, a downed pilot, and ten civilians. But this was the first time he'd been told about the medal.

Spencer stepped forward. "We waited to give it to you to make sure you were old enough to understand and appreciate how important it is, and responsible enough to value it and keep it safe."

"I am." J.J. looked up at Spencer. "And I will." Then he turned to Krissy. "Can I bring it into school for show and tell?"

With tears gathering in her eyes and emotion clogging her throat, all Krissy could do was nod.

Leave it to Spencer to clarify, "On a day either me, your mom, grandma or grandpa is available to bring it into school for you."

J.J. nodded.

Slowly he set down the box and picked up the

letter, staring at Jarrod's handwriting, like Krissy had done before opening and reading her own letter, like he'd done so many times since learning of the letter's existence.

He looked at Krissy for permission.

She nodded again.

A tear leaked down her cheek. If only Jarrod were here to see what a wonderful young man his son had turned out to be.

Spencer put a big, strong arm around her shoulders and held her close. Krissy looked over to see Bart doing the same to Patti, all eyes on J.J.

With the utmost care, J.J. used a letter opener to slowly and precisely slice open the top of the envelope, the ripping of paper the only sound in the room.

The envelope opened, J.J. reached in and removed the letter taking a quick look inside of the envelope before setting it down beside the box.

Then he climbed up on a stool in front of the counter, unfolded the letter and started to read. J.J. was at the top of his class in reading. Even so, Krissy couldn't help wondering if he'd be able to decipher Jarrod's handwriting, if he'd understand all of the words. He sat there reading, so quietly, not moving except when he finished one page and moved on to the next. Krissy could barely breathe, not knowing what Jarrod had written or how her son would react. The seconds ticked by like hours.

At one point J.J. smiled down at the letter, then he laughed, a snort-laugh, just like his father.

Then his face grew serious.

He sniffled.

Krissy wanted to run to him and comfort him. But when she made a move toward him, Spencer held her in place, shaking his head slightly. "He can handle it," Spencer whispered. So confident in the boy he'd raised as his own.

J.J. wiped his eyes then he smiled again and looked at Krissy. "Dad says hi. And that he loves you and wishes he could be here."

That's all it took. The tears she'd been trying to keep under control started to flow down her cheeks. She sucked in a hiccupping breath. Spencer rubbed her arms and kissed the top of her head.

"Oh." J.J. smiled. "He also said not to cry."

Krissy smiled through the tears.

"What else did he say," Patti asked, sounding hopeful.

J.J. jumped off of his stool and ran to Patti and Bart to give each one of them a hug. "That I have the best, most special grandparents in the whole world, which I already knew. And I should give each one of you a hug and kiss for him." Bart bent down for a kiss. Patti did the same. "He says he loves you."

That got Patti crying. Bart looked close to shedding a few tears, too.

J.J. walked over to Spencer, glanced at the letter and said, "Dad said you better be taking good care of me and teaching me to be a good man."

"Doing my best, buddy," Spencer said, messing up J.J.'s too long dark hair.

J.J. gave him a hug and Spencer bent down to squeeze him tight. The two of them shared such a close bond.

After releasing Spencer, J.J. walked back to the counter and dumped out the envelope. "Look," he said, holding up a baseball card. "My dad's favorite baseball card."

Bart said, "I was wondering what had happened to that. When he was young, like you, your dad used to sleep with it under his pillow hoping it'd make him a better baseball player."

J.J. seemed to like the sound of that. "I'm going to try that too."

Spencer whispered to Krissy, "It didn't work."

Krissy gave him a hip check.

"And look at this." J.J. held up a picture. "Dad in his uniform. A little one I can put in my wallet, someday, when I get a wallet. Like Dad has pictures of us in his wallet." J.J. held up the picture then read the back. "'To my special son. Love you always,'" he read. "'Dad.'"

Then J.J. held up a hundred dollar bill. "Dad says I can use this money to buy whatever I want, from him."

"You figure out what that is," Spencer said. "And I'll take you shopping."

"Thanks, Dad."

Sometimes it got confusing when J.J. talked about his dad, since he referred to both Jarrod and Spencer as Dad. Each held a special place in his heart, and each one was equally special to him, Krissy made sure of that.

J.J. started to fold up the letter.

"Wait," Krissy said. "That was a three-page letter. What else did he say?"

J.J. laughed. "Dad said you'd ask me that."

He knew her so well.

J.J. continued folding the letter and carefully slid it back into the envelope. "Private stuff. Just between me and him." He looked her straight in the eyes and made a threatening face. "Dad said to mind your own business and no snooping."

"What? I don't snoop!"

Spencer started to laugh. "Oh, yes, you do."

Yes. She did.

"You'd better hide it good, J.J.," Spencer teased.

"Oh, I will." Their son ran up the stairs heading toward his room.

"Traitor," Krissy said under her breath.

An hour later Krissy stood in her crowded, noisy living room watching J.J. tear into the rest of his presents, his eight-year-old brother and five-year-old sister helping like they had every right to be up front with him. They were such great children, all three of them. She'd been well and truly blessed.

Patti sat holding Kira's youngest, seven-year-old, Isabelle in her lap. Bart sat with his arm around Kira's oldest, nine-year-old, Kate. As far as Patti and Bart were concerned, they had five grandchildren, each one more special than the next. It seemed like Patti was always baking for some party or celebration and Bart took off the whole week leading up to Halloween to make sure everyone's costumes were just right, and attend all of the school parties, of course.

Spencer came to stand beside Krissy. "Penny for your thoughts?"

"Just thinking about how lucky I am and all Jarrod has given me." Patti and Bart, J.J. and Spencer and the two beautiful children she'd had with him.

Her handsome husband crossed his arms over his chest and said, "I'd like to think I had a little something to do with all this, too."

"You had *a lot* to do with it," she said. "But by asking me to have his baby if he didn't make it back from the war, and by making you the godfather of his baby, Jarrod brought you back into my life." Krissy wrapped her arms around his waist. "And Patti and Bart." And more love and happiness than Krissy had ever thought possible.

Spencer wrapped his arms around her shoulders. "Hard to believe how much my life has changed since you showed up at my door a little over ten years ago."

Krissy looked up at him. "I hope for the better."

Spencer leaned down to kiss her. "Definitely for the better." He hesitated. "Do you ever wonder what would have happened if Jarrod wasn't killed? If he'd come back a war hero? Would you have…?"

Krissy put her finger to Spencer's lips to stop him from talking. "I loved Jarrod. I still do. And I wish he could be here with us. But I never loved him, or any other man, for that matter, the way I love you. You're the only man for me," she told him, squeezing him tightly. "You poor thing." Sometimes her laid-back attitude drove him absolutely nuts.

"I love you, too," Spencer said. "And don't worry about me. I can handle you."

He could, better than anyone.

He leaned in close to whisper, "Tonight I plan to *handle you*…for hours."

Krissy smiled, so happy, and absolutely loving her life. "I can't wait."

* * * * *

MILLS & BOON®
Large Print Medical

March

A Daddy for Her Daughter	Tina Beckett
Reunited with His Runaway Bride	Robin Gianna
Rescued by Dr Rafe	Annie Claydon
Saved by the Single Dad	Annie Claydon
Sizzling Nights with Dr Off-Limits	Janice Lynn
Seven Nights with Her Ex	Louisa Heaton

April

Waking Up to Dr Gorgeous	Emily Forbes
Swept Away by the Seductive Stranger	Amy Andrews
One Kiss in Tokyo...	Scarlet Wilson
The Courage to Love Her Army Doc	Karin Baine
Reawakened by the Surgeon's Touch	Jennifer Taylor
Second Chance with Lord Branscombe	Joanna Neil

May

The Nurse's Christmas Gift	Tina Beckett
The Midwife's Pregnancy Miracle	Kate Hardy
Their First Family Christmas	Alison Roberts
The Nightshift Before Christmas	Annie O'Neil
It Started at Christmas...	Janice Lynn
Unwrapped by the Duke	Amy Ruttan

MILLS & BOON®
Large Print Medical

June

White Christmas for the Single Mum	Susanne Hampton
A Royal Baby for Christmas	Scarlet Wilson
Playboy on Her Christmas List	Carol Marinelli
The Army Doc's Baby Bombshell	Sue MacKay
The Doctor's Sleigh Bell Proposal	Susan Carlisle
Christmas with the Single Dad	Louisa Heaton

July

Falling for Her Wounded Hero	Marion Lennox
The Surgeon's Baby Surprise	Charlotte Hawkes
Santiago's Convenient Fiancée	Annie O'Neil
Alejandro's Sexy Secret	Amy Ruttan
The Doctor's Diamond Proposal	Annie Claydon
Weekend with the Best Man	Leah Martyn

August

Their Meant-to-Be Baby	Caroline Anderson
A Mummy for His Baby	Molly Evans
Rafael's One Night Bombshell	Tina Beckett
Dante's Shock Proposal	Amalie Berlin
A Forever Family for the Army Doc	Meredith Webber
The Nurse and the Single Dad	Dianne Drake

MILLS & BOON®
Large Print – March 2017

ROMANCE

Di Sione's Virgin Mistress	Sharon Kendrick
Snowbound with His Innocent Temptation	Cathy Williams
The Italian's Christmas Child	Lynne Graham
A Diamond for Del Rio's Housekeeper	Susan Stephens
Claiming His Christmas Consequence	Michelle Smart
One Night with Gael	Maya Blake
Married for the Italian's Heir	Rachael Thomas
Christmas Baby for the Princess	Barbara Wallace
Greek Tycoon's Mistletoe Proposal	Kandy Shepherd
The Billionaire's Prize	Rebecca Winters
The Earl's Snow-Kissed Proposal	Nina Milne

HISTORICAL

The Runaway Governess	Liz Tyner
The Winterley Scandal	Elizabeth Beacon
The Queen's Christmas Summons	Amanda McCabe
The Discerning Gentleman's Guide	Virginia Heath

MEDICAL

A Daddy for Her Daughter	Tina Beckett
Reunited with His Runaway Bride	Robin Gianna
Rescued by Dr Rafe	Annie Claydon
Saved by the Single Dad	Annie Claydon
Sizzling Nights with Dr Off-Limits	Janice Lynn
Seven Nights with Her Ex	Louisa Heaton

0217 GEN STD LP